"Ellie, are you positive your mother wrote this note?"

So he did think I skipped. I wanted to tell that I hadn't written the note, but I couldn't admit that Mom hadn't written it either. It was probably illegal for my brother Jake to write an excuse.

I hesitated. "That's her writing," I finally said.

"She typed it and signed it?" Mr. G. asked.

"She typed it," I said, without looking at him.

"Did you read it?" he asked.

"No."

He handed the note to me. It said, "Please excuse Ellie Brader's absence on Thursday and Friday due to a pooping fit." My mother's signature was written below.

"I think I still have the flu," I said. I thought I might throw up right on his desk.

Ellie Brader
Hates Mr. G.

Janet Johnston

A MINSTREL® BOOK

PUBLISHED BY POCKET BOOKS

New York   London   Toronto   Sydney   Tokyo   Singapore

This book is a work of fiction. Names, characters, places, and incidents are either the product of the author's imagination or are used fictitiously. Any resemblance to actual events or locales or persons, living or dead, is entirely coincidental.

 A Minstrel Book published by
POCKET BOOKS, a division of Simon & Schuster Inc.
1230 Avenue of the Americas, New York, NY 10020

Copyright © 1991 by Janet Johnston
Published by arrangement with Clarion Books, a Houghton Mifflin
Company imprint

ISBN: 0-671-78506-0

First Minstrel Book printing April 1995

10   9   8   7   6   5   4   3   2

A MINSTREL BOOK and colophon are registered trademarks
of Simon & Schuster Inc.

Cover art by Dan Burr

Printed in the U.S.A.

If you know the answer to the question, "What are you?" this book was written for you. And that's a fighters' promise.

Love,
Janny

Ellie Brader
Hates Mr. G.

I walked into Room 101 that morning and saw a substitute sitting at Ms. Simpson's desk. We'd had substitutes before in fifth grade, but Ms. Simpson had always told us about them ahead of time. She'd also told us that she wanted our behavior to be perfect for the substitute teacher.

"Remember," she'd say, "your behavior is a reflection on Thompson Elementary. You are all ambassadors."

This substitute was a surprise. She was taller and younger than Ms. Simpson, and I suppose she was prettier too, but I like the way Ms. Simpson looks.

I sat down in my seat and the woman looked at the seating chart in front of her.

"Are you Ellen Brader?" she asked.

"Yes. But people say Ellie."

"Fine. Ellie, will you please put one of these dittos on each desk?"

Her name was Ms. Brenslow. I sort of liked her, but she wasn't too smart. About four people told her wrong names, and Jenny and Beverly switched desks for the day. Every time she'd call on either one of them, the whole class would laugh.

Byron, who is the worst kid in class, told her that he had a disease that made him have to get a drink every twenty minutes.

"What disease is that?" she asked.

"My parents won't tell me," he said. "It's too horrible so they don't want me to know the name of it."

"Is it polio?" Maria asked, looking worried.

"No, Maria," Byron said. "It's not polio. That's cured. Don't you know anything?"

"That will do," Ms. Brenslow said. "Byron, you may get your drinks until lunchtime, at which point I'll check your medical record in the office."

"I don't think the school knows," Byron said. "Only Ms. Simpson knows. Is she sick today?"

"I don't know," Ms. Brenslow said. "I wasn't told."

"Maybe she has polio," Maria said.

"Let's stand for the pledge," Ms. Brenslow told us.

◆　◆　◆

It was my turn to set and clear the table that night and Jake's turn to wash the dishes. Jake is thirteen and in the eighth grade, but he's big for his age, so lots of people think he's about fifteen. My parents say that's a problem for him because people expect him to act older than he does. He acts about two years younger than I do most of the time.

I set the table perfectly for dinner. "Very nice, Ellie," my mother said, as we all sat down to eat. My mother cares a lot about how tables are set. Maybe that's why she opened a restaurant. She gets to set pretty many of them each day.

"We had a sub today," I said, while I waited for Jake to scoop tons of tuna casserole onto his plate.

"Where was Ms. Simpson?" Mom asked.

"The sub didn't know," I said. "I hope she's not sick."

"Maybe she died," Jake said.

Jake thinks that's a funny answer for anything, which shows how immature his sense of humor is.

"That's not funny, Jake," Mom told him.

"You know Byron?" I asked. "The bad kid? He told the sub that he had a disease and he had to get a drink of water every twenty minutes."

"Did she fall for it?" Jake wanted to know.

"I guess so, because she let him."

"That is so dumb," Jake said.

"What Byron did or what the sub did?" I asked.

"Pass the broccoli, please," Dad said. "I wouldn't be a substitute teacher for all the money in the world. Talk about a sentence."

"Were you mean to subs when you were in school?" I asked Dad.

"No. We were saints. We gave them the desserts out of our lunches."

Dad says things like that when he means the opposite. Now that I'm old enough to understand, I usually think they're funny.

After dinner I called Melissa Morrison, my best friend, to help me with spelling. She's in Room 101 too. She's in the high reading group with me, but she can spell, so her grades are a little higher than mine.

"Did you think that sub was pretty?" I asked her.

"Yes. But I like the way Ms. Simpson smiles better." We compared Ms. Simpson and the sub feature by feature, and we were onto hair when my father told me that he needed the phone. He's an accountant at Snelling and Bright and sometimes needs to make work calls at home. My mother talks forever to her restaurant partner, Flora Watson. The restaurant is only open for lunch. I can't imagine how long they'd talk if they served breakfast and dinner too.

"Got to go," I told Melissa. "Robert needs the phone." Melissa and I call our own and each other's parents by their first names, but never when they can hear us. It's like a secret joke.

"That's okay," Melissa said. "Gayle wants me to walk the dog." Gayle is Ms. Morrison. "Tell Robert hi. See you tomorrow in school."

Dad came and stood beside me to let me know that I'd better hang up immediately.

"Melissa says hi," I told him, replacing the receiver.

"Oh." He looked surprised. "That's nice."

After dinner I got to walk Willie, our dog, while Jake washed dishes. Willie is medium-sized and he's white with black spots. That makes him sound like a Dalmatian, but he's fluffy and only has about eight large spots. We got him at the animal shelter. All you have to pay for there is the shots that the dog gets. You buy the shots, and they throw the dog in free. It's a great deal.

I knew Jake wished he could be walking Willie instead of doing dishes. I was glad it was my turn and not his. As I was leaving the kitchen, I said sweetly, "Tell Jake bye-bye, Willie. Tell Jake you'll miss him."

"That's so dumb," Jake said.

"He says you're dumb, Willie. I'm sorry you had to hear that."

"Ellie," Mom said, coming into the kitchen, "get going, so you'll have time for homework."

"I'm leaving, Mom," I said, in my fake sweet voice. "Jake's pet just wanted to tell him good-bye."

"Ellie." Mom's voice was a warning. She knew I was trying to annoy Jake.

"I'm gone," I said, opening the back door. "Jake's sorry, Willie," I added before I shut it behind me.

I smiled at the thought of Jake saying "That's so dumb" to the dishes he was washing.

❖ ❖ ❖

We had another substitute on Tuesday and then a different one on Wednesday. On Wednesday afternoon a note went home to the parents saying that Ms. Simpson would not be back for the rest of the school year, which was the last eight weeks of school—almost a whole marking period. The note said that Ms. Simpson's mother was gravely ill in Rhode Island and that Ms. Simpson had taken emergency leave to remain with her.

When we walked home that day, Melissa told me that she felt like crying. I did too. I hated carrying the note home in my backpack. Melissa and I walked silently. Her black, curly hair bounced with each step, and it seemed odd for her hair to look so happy when her dark eyes looked so sad.

"Stupid Byron said that he won't miss her," Melissa said after a while.

"I'll bet he's just lying. He really likes her. Look at that tray he gave her at Christmas."

"We'll never have another teacher that nice."

"I know," I said. "Do you think she'll come back for next year?"

"I guess. I don't know. Maybe by that time her mother will be well."

I wondered if her mother might die, but I was too sad to say it. I couldn't think about how Ms. Simpson would feel if her mother died. "I wish this hadn't happened," I said. "I wish everything had stayed regular until the end of the year. And her mother never got sick at all."

"Me too," Melissa said. "I'll call you tonight." She turned up her street.

◆　◆　◆

Mom was still at the restaurant when I got home. I decided that Ms. Simpson's mother was an emergency, so I called Mom at work. Ms. Watson answered. "Is my mother there?" I asked.

"She's on her way home now," she said. "How was school?"

"Fine," I said, which was a lie, but I don't count those kinds as bad.

Jake got home before Mom did. He looked at my honey-and-peanut-butter sandwich. "How about making me one?" he asked.

"Why should I?" I asked back.

"Why shouldn't you?" he answered, as he got out the honey and peanut butter and started his own sandwich. I knew I'd been mean, and I wished I'd made the sandwich, or at least answered him in a nicer way.

"Ms. Simpson won't be back for the rest of the year," I told him.

"So she *did* die," he said.

"You dumb baby!" I said, but I started to cry in

the middle of saying it, so I ran upstairs. I should have known better than to tell him something important.

I lay down on my bed and held my hen. It's a stuffed hen that I got years ago, and it's pretty messy. I used to chew on its beak, so that's gone, and the eyes fell off a long time ago. I still keep it on my bed, because I still love it.

I heard Mom come in downstairs and talk to Jake. Soon she opened my door.

"Hi," she said, sitting down on the bed. "What's the problem?"

"What did Jake say?"

"That you were upset about your teacher."

I knew Jake hadn't said that. He probably said I was being a hyper baby. Mom tries to cover up the fact that he's a creep, probably hoping that he'll outgrow it.

"I have a school note," I said.

"What does it say?"

"Ms. Simpson won't be back for the year." I could feel myself almost crying again so I squeezed my hen.

"Oh, Ellie, that's too bad." She rubbed my back. "I know you must feel sad. *I* feel sad. Do you know why she's gone?"

"Her mother's gravely ill in Rhode Island."

"Oh, I see. Do you know who your new teacher will be?"

"No. The sub today said that she'd finish the week,

then the permanent teacher would start. But I want Ms. Simpson."

"Of course you do. When you're with someone that many hours a day and you care for them, it's hard not to see them. Would you like to write her a letter?"

"I don't know where her mother lives."

"We can find out the address. I'll find it for you. I'm sure she'd love to hear from you. She must miss everyone, besides being worried about her mother."

"All right. Should I use lined paper or stationery?"

"Why don't we buy a special card?"

"Tonight?"

"Yes. I've got to get Jake's shoes at the mall, so we can get the card then."

"All right."

After my mother left, I rested for a while longer. I felt better. Mom has heart-to-heart talks with Jake and me if we're in trouble or if we're sad. The trouble ones can be a pain, because they're long, but the sad ones help.

At the mall we bought a card for Ms. Simpson. I chose one that had pansies on the front because she once said that pansies are her favorite flowers. They're my favorite, too, because of the faces, not because of Ms. Simpson.

When we got home from the mall, I wrote my pansies card. I used my best penmanship and I asked my mother the words I couldn't spell. For a change, she just told me the spelling without the rules.

"Do you think I should say *love?*" I asked her.

"You mean like, *Love, Ellie?*"

"Yes."

"Of course," she said. "Why not?"

"Well, I don't know if it's proper."

"It's always proper when you love someone," Mom said.

I'd never thought about loving Ms. Simpson. Usually just kindergarten kids think they love their teachers. Or maybe only kindergarten kids admit it. I thought I might love Ms. Simpson. I'd never tell anyone though. But I wrote "Love, Ellie" on my card. I knew that Ms. Simpson would probably understand. She was good at getting things.

I wondered if the new teacher would be.

2

*B*efore school started on Monday, all we could talk about was getting a new teacher.

"I hope we get that first substitute," Sue Ann said.

"It can't be a sub, remember?" I said. "That second one said so."

"Well," Sue Ann said, "I liked that first woman's shoes. Didn't you, Melissa?"

"I don't remember them," Melissa said.

"You must be kidding," Sue Ann said, acting shocked.

Everything is either too funny or too shocking or too something for Sue Ann. She annoyed me. But she didn't seem to annoy Melissa.

"What did they look like?" Melissa asked her.

"Blue with metal dots. They were very stylish."

"Want to play tetherball?" Melissa asked us both.

"Sure," I said.

"I'll play for a minute," Sue Ann said. "If I get sweaty, my curls will come out, and I'll feel messy all day."

When we walked into Room 101, there were two men standing by the door. One was Mr. Teal, the principal of Thompson Elementary. The other man was even older than Mr. Teal.

"Class, please be seated," Mr. Teal said.

Everyone was quiet. You have to be quiet to hear Mr. Teal. He has a Southern accent and he speaks very softly. We used to call him Quack Quack (not to his face) because of teal duck, but then last year Bennet started calling him Quiet Quack, and now we all call him that.

"Class," Mr. Teal said, "I have the distinct pleasure of presenting your new teacher, Mr. Garrett, to all of you."

I had never imagined a man teacher to replace Ms. Simpson. This man could have been her grandfather. He had white hair and he looked serious, like a television newscaster.

Quiet Quack kept speaking. "Mr. Garrett has taught in our school system for many years. In fact, he retired just last year, and we persuaded him to come back to help you people finish up your last quarter. I know you will help him learn the program here at Thompson."

I didn't want to help him. I didn't even want him to

be in our room trying to take Ms. Simpson's place. I glanced over at Melissa. She caught my eye and shook her head no, the tiniest bit. I knew what she meant. No to Mr. Garrett, no to Ms. Simpson being gone for good, no to the whole thing.

Jenny was staring at her desk as she rubbed her finger around and around the outside of the pencil indentation. Sue Ann was watching Mr. Garrett closely and smiling.

Check out those shoes, Sue Ann, I thought.

"Good morning," Mr. Garrett said. "If you will excuse me, I need to step out into the hall for a moment with Mr. Teal, and then we can begin." He sounded like a serious newscaster too.

Both men walked out and closed the door behind them.

"Gross!" Byron said. "He's ancient. He's a dinosaur."

"He's not that old," Maria said.

"He's twice as old as Quiet Quack," Byron told her.

Jenny and Beverly jumped up and exchanged desks, giggling.

"He's not as old as the music teacher," Maria was saying.

"You're nuts," Byron said. "He's a dinosaur." Then Byron howled "Tyrannosaurus rex." He did it over and over. When he said *rex*, he tilted his face back and opened his mouth as wide as he could (which is wide).

Somehow, because he's so fat, it was very ugly to watch.

Bruce, the second worst kid in class, began to pound on his desk.

Mr. Garrett opened the door, looked around the instantly quiet room, then closed the door again.

"He didn't even say anything," Sue Ann said.

"No," Byron agreed. "That's weird. Even Mr. Teal would have quacked."

Mr. Garrett opened the door again and came into the room. He crossed in front of the board and stopped behind Ms. Simpson's desk. It made me sad to see him there and know that she really wasn't coming back for the rest of the year.

"Let us begin by—" Mr. Garrett said. Byron raised his hand. "Yes?" Mr. Garrett said to Byron.

"Mr. Garrett," Byron said in his fake good-kid voice, "I've got a serious disease and I have to get a drink of water every ten minutes."

Mr. Garrett just stared at him without answering.

"Or else something serious will happen," Byron added.

"And what might that be?"

Byron hesitated. "I don't know. Every teacher lets me get my drinks, so I don't know what would happen."

"Well, today we'll find out, won't we?" Mr. Garrett said, picking up the seating chart.

This teacher is seriously mean, I thought.

"Maria Randolph," he said, looking at the first desk, where Maria sat.

"Present," she answered.

"So I see," he said. "Kevin Ashurst."

When he got to Beverly Beaumont's desk, he called out her name and Jenny answered. Her voice was serious but a few people giggled. He stared at Jenny, then said again, "Beverly Beaumont."

By this time, Jenny's face was bright red and she looked sick. "Present," she said again in a whispery voice.

He looked back at the seating chart, then said, "And what's your middle name, Beverly Beaumont?"

Even Jenny's neck was red. "I don't know," she said, staring at the desk top.

"Well, then, do you know where your actual seat is?" he asked.

Jenny and Beverly stood at the same time and went quickly to their own seats.

"Beverly Lynn Beaumont," Mr. Garrett said.

"Present," Beverly answered.

He continued to call the roll.

◆ ◆ ◆

The lunch line stretched all the way to the gym door because we were having pizza. Most people buy on pizza day and practically no one buys on fish day. Melissa and I both were buying lunch.

"I think Mr. Garrett's mean, really mean," I told Melissa while we waited for our food.

"He's strict," she said. "Superstrict. I can't tell about mean yet."

"He was mean to Jenny. She almost cried."

"But she changed desks, and that's something you only do to subs, really," Melissa said.

"Yeah, but I think he was mean to her."

"How did he know for sure that Byron didn't have to drink water?" Melissa asked.

"I don't know. But what if he really had to?"

"Then it could have been an emergency," she said. "If Byron had died, his parents could sue Mr. Garrett."

"They'd probably give him a present."

"*I'd* give him one," Melissa said, picking up her tray. "He won't be like Ms. Simpson."

"No. No one could be as good as she was. But I'd rather have one of those substitutes, I think."

"Do you wish we didn't have a man?" Melissa asked.

"Yes. The boys will think he'll be easy on them and mean to us."

"I don't think he'll be easy on anyone," Melissa said.

"I know. I wish it were summer already."

◆　◆　◆

"Before we get to our leaf projects," Mr. Garrett said, after lunch, "we need to do some organizational chores."

Jenny and I glanced at each other, and she shrugged her shoulders quickly as if to say, "I don't know what he means."

"By this I mean," he continued, "that we're beyond some of the organizational controls that we now have in place. For example, we are no longer going to have line leaders."

I stared at him. I was the line leader for the rest of the week. The whole year's line leaders and helping hands were all arranged on tags. Ms. Simpson did that before school even started. Now, I was not only losing my line leadership, but the whole rest of the class who hadn't had their second turns wouldn't get them. It wasn't fair.

Sue Ann raised her hand. "Mr. Garrett, Ms. Simpson said that if there were certain line leaders, it would cut down on fighting about who gets to go first."

"Perhaps there were fights about such things at the beginning of the year," he answered. "After all, you were basically fourth-graders. Now you are almost sixth-graders. Sixth-graders do not fight about who gets to go first."

Jenny, Sue Ann, and the rest of the people who hadn't been line leaders looked at each other. Byron, who had been the line leader, smirked happily. He'd had his turn.

"And next," Mr. Garrett said, "we need to add a homework policy. If you come to school without your homework assignment, you will stay in the classroom and clean the boards during recess. If you don't bring the paper the next day, you'll miss recess and stay after school as well. On that day your parents will also be called. Any questions?"

Melissa's hand was up first. "What if you did it but just forgot it?"

"The two parts of an assignment are doing it and bringing it. If you didn't bring it, you didn't complete the entire assignment. Other questions?"

The room was silent.

"We also need to discuss Bingo," Mr. Garrett said. The sun bounced off his white hair as he glanced down at a card and made a mark. He probably checked off, *Line leaders, fired,* and *Boards, cleaned.*

"I want to alter the policy on Bingo somewhat," he said, and all eyes in the room turned toward Bingo's cage.

Bingo was the class rabbit. He was black with a little bit of dark brown over his back legs and on his tail, and dark-brown eyes. He was a beautiful rabbit.

Ms. Simpson brought him into our classroom during the second week of school. It took us almost an hour that day to name him. Everyone had different ideas about what he should be called. Sue Ann wanted to call him Precious. That nearly made me sick. The whole class argued and voted and changed votes until Ms. Simpson said that if we couldn't come to an agreement, she wouldn't let us vote until the next day. No one wanted the rabbit to be nameless overnight, and finally Bruce bossed people into agreeing on Bingo, which was his choice and, from him, not bad.

I had no idea what horrible plan Mr. Garrett had for Bingo. I was afraid that he'd stop letting people take Bingo home, just as he'd stopped having line leaders. Since Bingo came to Room 101, we took turns feeding him each week, and on the week you fed him you also got to take him home for the weekend if you brought a note from a parent. If you weren't allowed to take him home, Ms. Simpson took him. Only two people hadn't been allowed to take him home. Wallace couldn't because if his sister breathed Bingo's fur she could die, and Shannon couldn't because her father was mean. Her mother wanted Bingo, she even sent a note saying so, but her father sent another one saying no. I had taken Bingo home once already, and my turn came up again soon.

"The only modification in the rabbit policy," Mr. Garrett said, "will involve the end of the year. To be in the drawing for the rabbit, you need only to want him and to have a note from a parent."

Groans from around the room mixed with cheers. I groaned. My chance to win was instantly smaller. Many people's chances were smaller. Ms. Simpson's rule had been that a person must have a B or better in conduct to participate in the drawing, which would be held on the last day of school.

This time Jenny tried to talk to Mr. Garrett.

"Mr. Garrett, Ms. Simpson said that Bingo would be the reward for good conduct in the classroom. For someone who had good conduct all year."

He looked at Jenny, not in a mean way, not in a friendly way—he just looked. "I don't reward good conduct," he finally said. "I expect it. But every teacher is different."

Yeah, I thought, some are better.

Of course, Bruce and Byron and everyone else with rotten conduct were smiling the whole time. Even they had to know that it wasn't fair. A lot of us had worked all year for good conduct grades just to have a chance to get Bingo, and now there would be tons more people in the drawing, people who hadn't even tried at all. If they'd really wanted the rabbit, they'd have shown it by their conduct grades. I thought it was awful.

Walking home from school, Sue Ann told Melissa and me that she was shocked about the rabbit change, and for once I agreed with her. It was shocking.

◆ ◆ ◆

I told my parents about it at dinner.

"We have a man teacher and no one likes him," I

said. "His name's Mr. Garrett and he's unfair and mean."

"Aren't you judging a little quickly?" my mother asked.

"No," I said. "We had him all day."

"Then by all means, you're in a position to decide," Dad said, cutting his meat loaf.

"Well, he did enough in one day to make everyone mad," I said.

"Like what?" Jake asked.

I explained the new rules on Bingo.

"I don't think that's bad," my mother said. "Imagine how the students with lower grades would have felt during the drawing."

"Mom, it's not like work grades. I know that work grades wouldn't have been fair, because everyone is different in what they're smart at. Maria's not very smart in school but she tries hard and gets perfect conduct grades. Those kids could have tried too. What if Bruce gets him? Or fat Byron?"

"He'll eat him," Jake said.

"Curb it," Dad told him, but Dad was smiling.

"Well, I don't think it's funny," I said. "I worked all year on my conduct grades to get a chance to keep Bingo, and now this *dinosaur* changes everything."

"Ellie, do not call your teacher names. It sounds bratty," Mom said.

"She *is* bratty," Jake said.

"Last chance, Jake," my father said. This time he wasn't smiling.

I stood up. "May I be excused?" I asked. "I've finished eating and it's not my turn to wash."

"I suppose so," my mother said. I left the room and started upstairs, but I could hear Mom talking.

"Jake, Ellie feels bad about Ms. Simpson. Try to be a little more understanding, okay?"

"Dibs on her dessert," he said.

He really is a creep.

3

We had our health essay test on Wednesday, and as we finished we were allowed to work on individual projects in the room. Ms. Simpson had started lots of individual art projects before she left.

I went to the back to work with Dawn and Jenny on the wagon train mural. Our class had been working on it for about three weeks and it was almost finished. Dawn did a lot of the drawing and the rest of us painted the colors in. She's great on horses and people. We all added trees, rocks, and scenery, and Jenny drew most of the outlines for the wagons. The only thing that wasn't perfect was that Maria's trees looked just like broccoli, and Byron added smiley faces (the only thing he can draw) in odd places. There was one smiley face riding on a wagon and another one peeking out from behind a cactus. It was dumb.

Dawn and Jenny and I were working on filling in the sky. We were making a sunset. Dawn showed us how to keep adding water to blend the colors. "You want them to hook together but stay their own colors," she said.

Dawn has long blond hair that is wavy like mermaid hair, and her hair kept touching the wet painting, which made the ends of her curls turn pink. I was looking at her hair when I reached across the mural for the cup of purple paint. My hand hit the side of the cup, and suddenly the paint was making a widening puddle all over the class mural.

"Oh, I'm sorry!" I said, as the watery paint covered wagon after wagon.

Byron turned around in his seat. "Way to ruin the mural, Ellie," he yelled.

"What's the problem?" Mr. Garrett asked, coming to the back of the room.

"We spilled the paint," Jenny said, as she tried to blot up some of the huge puddle with paper towels.

"I did it," I said quietly.

Mr. Garrett looked at the mural. "You'll need to throw it away," he said, "and then go on to the restroom to get cleaned up." He went back up front to help Maria.

Jenny, Dawn, and I rolled the mural up. Everyone kept looking back at us. The rude kids groaned and made comments, and the nice ones just looked sad. I was afraid I was going to cry in front of everyone.

Dawn went to the nurse's room bathroom because she had paint on her dress and the nurse has clothes-washing soap. Jenny and I went to clean up in the bathroom near our classroom. As soon as we walked in I went into one of the cubicles and closed the door and started to cry. I tried to be quiet because I didn't want Jenny to hear me. She had the water running so she could clean up. After a while the water was turned off and she said, "Will you be ready to go back pretty soon?"

I made my voice sound as regular as I could. "You go ahead. I'll be there soon."

"I'll wait for you," she said.

"I need to get cleaned up," I answered.

"I'll help you," she said.

I wiped my eyes and opened the bathroom door. "I think I'm getting a cold," I told her.

"You should take vitamins. I do. No one will know you were crying after you wash your face," she added.

I started to cry again. "It was my fault. And everyone's work is gone. But Mr. Garrett doesn't have to be so mean. Ms. Simpson would have said that it was all right and stuff. You know."

Jenny nodded and her straight brown hair brushed against her shoulders. "She would have. But I think he just thinks it's better to get stuff taken care of. I don't know."

I went over to the sink and began washing tears off

my face and purple paint off my arms. "I *really* miss Ms. Simpson," I said.

"So do I," Jenny said. "Come on. I'll French-braid your hair before we go back. It'll make you feel better."

It sounded silly, but she was right.

◆　◆　◆

In the middle of the night, I found out by surprise that I had the flu. I woke up and had to go to the bathroom, and as I walked down the hall all of a sudden I had to throw up so fast that I thought I wouldn't make it. It was as if I caught the flu right in the middle of the hall. After I threw up the first time, I went to tell Mom that I was sick. I ended up staying home for two days plus the weekend.

As I got better, I got bored, so I wanted to go back to school. What I didn't want was to go back to school and see Mr. Garrett instead of Ms. Simpson.

By Monday, I was well enough to go. The alarm clock didn't go off, and everyone was running late. My mom always gets mad when she hurries.

"Someone get the dog fed," she said. "And the trash should have been emptied last night. You two are going to have to start setting your own clocks."

"I need an excuse," I said.

"Nuts, that's right. Jake, type an excuse for Ellie and I'll sign it. The new pastry chef is going to be there waiting to get in."

When Jake was little, Dad let him play with an old typewriter, and Jake learned to type. He doesn't hit the right keys with the right fingers, Dad says, but he types for real and pretty fast. I got to play with that same typewriter, but I can't type. I'm not sure why.

Mom signed the note, I fed Willie, Jake took out the trash, and finally we all left for the day.

I met Melissa halfway to school. It seemed as if I hadn't seen her for a long time, as if I hadn't been out of the house for at least a week.

"Are you better now?" she asked.

"Yes. But milk still tastes funny. What happened in school while I was gone?"

"Nothing. We're on Quebec. And Brenda got her hair cut. It's kind of like Joan's now. I like it."

"Was anyone else absent?"

"Just Byron one day. He probably skipped."

"Yeah."

"Yesterday I bought lunch," Melissa said, "and Byron ate five pieces of pizza. He just kept going back with more money."

"What a tank."

"Sue Ann thought maybe you were faking being sick. But I told her you had the flu."

"I wonder if Mr. Garrett thinks I was faking."

"No. He just takes roll. I don't think he thinks about it."

◆   ◆   ◆

Brenda's hair looked nice. When I told her that it was pretty she smiled and said, "My mother made me do it, but it's okay."

After the pledge Mr. Garrett asked me, "Did you bring a note today?"

I had forgotten to give it to him when I came in. "Yes," I said, and I took it out of my pocket. I looked at Sue Ann to make sure she noticed when I walked up to Mr. Garrett's desk.

I stood there as he read the note. He seemed to take an awfully long time to get through it. The notes that Jake and I bring are always the same: "Please excuse Ellie Brader's (or Jake Brader's) absence on blank day due to illness." Mom writes in the correct date.

After a long time, Mr. Garrett said, "You may be seated," and this time when I walked past Sue Ann she stared at her book. She might have been sorry that she told Melissa I skipped. She should have been sorry.

◆ ◆ ◆

Melissa was going to save me a place at lunch. The people who buy lunch go down first to get in line and the ones who bring lunch join them later.

I was picking up my lunch box to leave when Mr. Garrett said, "I'd like to see you for a moment, Ellie."

A few kids turned to look at me as they walked out of the room.

I thought Mr. Garrett was going to give me makeup

work from when I was absent. But when I stepped up to his desk, he took a green paper out of a folder. I recognized my excuse.

"Ellie," he said, "are you positive that your mother wrote this note?"

So he did think I skipped. I wanted to tell him that I hadn't written the note, but I couldn't admit that Mom hadn't written it either. It was probably illegal for Jake to write an excuse.

I hesitated before answering. "That's her writing," I finally said.

"She typed it and signed it?" he asked.

Would I get expelled from school because of this? I wondered. Would something happen to Mom for letting Jake write it? Would Jake get expelled too? I was starting to feel sick again.

"She typed it," I said, without looking at him.

"Did you read it?" he asked.

"No."

He handed the note to me. It said, "Please excuse Ellie Brader's absence on Thursday and Friday due to a pooping fit." My mother's signature was written below.

"I think I still have the flu," I said. I thought I might throw up right on his desk.

"You may go to lunch," he said. "And if you feel sick, you can notify your parents, or else the nurse can do it for you."

I nodded and walked out of the classroom.

I went straight to the office and asked to use the phone. It was the nice secretary. "Sure, honey," she said.

The mean one always says, "Two minutes."

I dialed the restaurant number and my mom answered. I tried to talk quietly so the secretary wouldn't hear.

"Mom, Jake wrote *pooping fit* on my excuse. That's what he put. And you signed it. I gave it to Mr. Garrett and he thinks it wasn't you, but I lied and said it was, because I thought he thought I did it. I want you to come and get me. I can't go back and see him. I hate Jake. I hate him for life. I do." I started to cry.

"Ellie, wait. Wait a minute." I could hear the restaurant music and people talking. "Ellie, what did you lie about?" she asked.

"Mom, my lying is not as bad as what Jake did!"

"I just need to know what's happening."

"I told Mr. Garrett I was sick, but I'm not. I just can't go back there. He thinks I wrote a note that said I had a pooping fit. Or else he thinks you wrote it."

"Are you sure the note said that?" she asked.

"Yes. He gave it to me to read."

"Damn. I can't believe Jake would do that and let you take it. I can't believe I didn't catch it." She stopped talking for a second. "Ellie, you'll have to go back. I'll come when school is out and explain what happened."

"No, no, because I lied and then he'll know."

"He already knows," she said. "Or else he thinks your mother is demented. Jake did it, not you. I'll explain it."

"Mom, no, please! I'll stay here but don't come."

"Ellie, it would be best—"

"Please, Mom. Please."

"All right. We'll talk about it tonight. I'll see you at home."

When I finally got to the cafeteria, lunch period was almost over. I couldn't stand to tell anyone what happened, even Melissa, so I just didn't talk much.

In the classroom, Mr. Garrett said, "Are you feeling better?" as I walked past his desk to put my lunch box away. I nodded, and the rest of the day went on as usual, except it seemed hours and hours long.

Neither car was in the driveway when I got home so I knew Mom wasn't there yet. I kept hoping that she hadn't broken her word and gone to school. Sometimes she thinks she has to do something for my own good. I hoped this wasn't one of those times.

I was sitting on the couch when Jake came in. He looked at me and threw his books down and said, "I see the shrimp boat arrived."

"I hate you," I told him.

He looked surprised. "Gee, thanks. Who jerked your chain?"

"I gave your note to Mr. Garrett. And now I'll probably get kicked out of school."

"Now what?" he asked, but before I could answer

he said, "Oh, no! You didn't!" He wasn't laughing, and he didn't have his mean look on. He looked scared, scared and sad.

"Why did you do it?" I asked him.

"I was joking. I was teasing. I thought Mom would read it and screech at me and then I'd just type it right."

"Well, why didn't you?"

"I don't know. She didn't yell, and then I got busy and forgot. Oh, grim. Ellie, I'm sorry."

That was the first time in Jake's life that he ever told me he was sorry without having been made to say it by Mom or Dad. I could tell he was honestly sorry. It was kind of amazing.

"What did your teacher say?" he asked.

"He thought Mom didn't write it."

"So what did you say?" he asked.

"I said she did," I told him.

"You said she wrote that? Why?"

"Well, what do you expect? It might be against the law for you to do it. I thought Mom might get in trouble or you might get kicked out of school."

Jake groaned. "Oh, grim," he said again. "Have you told Mom or Dad? We've got to tell them right away. And I'm a dead man."

"I told Mom. I called her at work during lunch."

"What did she say?"

"She swore," I said.

"On the phone? To you? At school?"

I nodded.

"You're looking at a dead man," he said.

"I think so too," I told him.

"Did she call your teacher?" he asked.

"No. I begged her not to. She was going to go there after work. I'm still afraid she might."

"Well, she has to. He has to know. He can't just think Mom wrote it. She'd have to be nuts."

"Maybe he thinks I did it."

"That's worse. He'll have to know it was me."

"But I lied," I said. "I told him about three times that Mom wrote the note before I saw it."

"But still. That's because you didn't know what else to do. How often would something like this come up? Dad's going to kill me."

We both heard the car pull into the driveway. The car door slammed extra hard, and Jake closed his eyes and made a face at the sound. The kitchen door opened.

"Jake? Ellie?" Mom called.

"We're in here," I said. Jake didn't answer.

Mom walked into the living room and I could tell that she was furious, because her face was bright red.

"Young man," she said, "did your sister tell you what happened?"

"Yes," Jake said.

"If she hadn't read the note with her own eyes, I'd swear it wasn't true. That's how sure I was you wouldn't do anything so stupid."

"Mom, I—"

"Why on earth would you do such a thing?"

"I thought that—"

"Don't you realize the position this puts your sister in? The whole family in?"

"Not Dad," Jake said.

"What?" Mom yelled.

"I just mean that he didn't sign it. The teacher probably thinks Dad's regular."

"Well, he certainly doesn't think I'm regular," Mom said. "Why did you do it?"

"I thought you'd see it and just get shook and Ellie would have a fit and then I'd write it right."

"But why did you let her take it?"

"I didn't mean for her to. I forgot about it when I was looking for my science book, and then you never screeched so I wasn't reminded."

"I didn't screech," Mom said, "because I thought I was signing something that my son was mature enough to write. So I didn't check. And neither did Ellie. We depended on you."

Both Mom and Jake looked as though they were going to cry. My throat was starting to hurt terribly.

"He didn't mean to," I said. "He didn't mean for this to happen."

I heard Dad's car in the driveway.

"Does Dad know?" Jake asked Mom.

"Yes," she said. "I called him at work."

Jake was pale. I was beginning to feel really sorry for him.

Dad came in the front door and looked at all of us.

"Did you go to school?" he asked Mom.

"No," she said.

"Good," he answered, and then he turned to Jake. He held out a piece of paper, which Jake took without looking up. "This is Mr. Garrett's address and phone number," Dad said. "It's close enough for you to go on your bike. Or you can call. This situation is your responsibility. You fix it before dinner. Is that clear?"

Jake nodded and walked upstairs.

"But what'll Jake say?" I asked my father. "I don't want Mr. Garrett to know I lied."

"It can't be helped."

He walked over and kissed my mother. "Think of it this way," he told her. "If it happened to someone else, you'd think it was funny."

"Not if I liked them," Mom said, putting her head on Dad's shoulder.

I decided to set the table, even though it wasn't my turn.

4

Jake called Mr. Garrett on the phone because he thought that was less scary than going in person. He told us about it at dinner. He said he didn't ride over because his bike tire was low, but I knew it was because he was scared. I didn't blame him. I would have been scared too.

"Who answered?" I asked him.

"He did. And he didn't sound friendly. He said he'd assumed that something of the sort had happened. Then he asked to talk to Mom or Dad."

"Why did you pick Mom?" I asked,

"I wondered that too," Mom said.

"Because you were right there in the hall with Ellie," Jake told her. "I thought maybe you were trying to listen."

"Of course not," Mom said. "I was straightening the linen closet."

I had been trying to listen, but Jake was talking too softly.

"So what did he say?" Dad asked her.

"Well," she told Dad, "he said that the incident was our fault, not Jake's, and that if we'd complied with school rules, it wouldn't have happened." Mom was talking the way she does when she'd rather be saying it to Dad alone. I thought maybe she was mad at Mr. Garrett and trying not to show it.

"So, are you on academic probation?" Dad asked.

"I don't think that's funny, Robert. He's right. As he said, the school policy states that a parent will write an excuse for a child, but we allowed Jake to do it."

"That's true," Jake said.

"Listen," Dad said to Jake, "he may be right that according to the school rules, we should have written the note. But according to this family's rules, if one of us asks you to do something, we don't expect you to goof it up."

"He *is* right, though, Robert," Mom said again.

"I suppose he is," Dad said.

"Is he strict at school?" Mom asked.

"Yes," I said. "He's mean. Not like Ms. Simpson."

"No reason why he should be," Dad said. "In general, I prefer strict teachers anyway."

"He shouldn't say stuff to Mom about what to do," I said.

"No, Ellie," Mom said. "If parents go against school policy in some way, it's his job to tell them. If we let you be late for school every day, he'd talk to us about it."

"Ms. Simpson wasn't that way," I said. "Two times, Becky's mom was supposed to send brownies for a party and she forgot, and Ms. Simpson just acted nice about it."

"That's different," Mom said. "Brownies aren't a school rule."

"Ellie's right," Jake said. "He's a grouch award candidate."

"Well," Mom said, "he probably wouldn't give you the greatest conduct grades at this point either."

"Pass the coleslaw," Jake said.

The blue bowl of coleslaw was closest to Mom, but she acted as if she didn't hear him.

"Please," Jake added.

She handed him the bowl.

◆ ◆ ◆

I thought Mr. Garrett might speak to me about what had happened when I saw him the next day at school, but he didn't. I knew he was wrong to blame Mom and Dad. Jake wrote the note and I lied about it. I didn't think Mr. Garrett was being fair to say it was my parents' fault. I felt sad in the classroom, as if I didn't belong there, as if 101 weren't my real room anymore.

◆ ◆ ◆

Melissa was coming to spend the night on Friday. It rained all day on Friday and Melissa's mother brought her to my house in the car.

It was still raining after dinner when Melissa and I started the fudge. We were going to make a double batch because we'd asked Mom, Dad, and Jake if they wanted any, and they all said they did.

While the candy cooked, we told each other's fortunes about four times. You have to name six boys, six places, and six of everything else (like numbers of children you want). Then you find out who you'll marry and where you'll live and how many children you'll have.

Twice it came up that I was going to marry Wallace.

"Do you like him?" Melissa asked.

"No!" I said. "He's gross."

"Then why did you put his name first each time?"

"I just thought of it because he sits near me."

"I'll bet you like him. I like Joey a little. Not much."

"Joey in Ms. Bently's class?"

"Yes. Just a little."

"Why?" Joey is tiny, much tinier than Melissa, and everyone calls him the Frog.

"He's nice," she said. "He lets me have cuts in teth-erball."

I had to think about it. I'd never thought of the Frog as someone Melissa might like.

"So do you like Wallace?" she asked.

"Maybe," I said. "Just a teeny tiny bit. And you can never tell. Promise?"

"Yes. Do you promise not to tell about Joey?"

"Yes," I said. "I like the way Wallace talks," I added. Wallace came to our school last year. He has an accent because he's from Alabama. It sounds nice.

While the fudge cooled, we started talking about school food and which meal was the worst.

Barbecued chicken is my grossest meal. The sauce is too thin, so it looks like bare chicken, and you can see dots on the wings where the feathers were. Byron calls it sunburned chicken but that doesn't stop him from eating a ton of it.

"That salmon stuff is worse than sunburned chicken," Melissa said. "It tastes like cat food."

"But Byron eats it," I told her. "I've seen him."

"He'd eat it if it were cat food," she said.

"Would cat food make someone sick?" I asked her.

"No. Because cats can eat people food too. Cats and people can switch back and forth on their food."

"Then I'm going to make Byron a cat-food sand-wich," I said.

She smiled. "You know he wouldn't eat it. Not even Byron would eat that."

I'd been joking, but all of sudden I realized how the trick could work. "What if he didn't know?"

"That would be so funny," she said. "And get him back for all the mean things he's done. Especially to Maria. But I don't see how you can get him to eat it."

"I'll trade it to him," I said. "I'll make him beg to trade it."

She started to laugh. "That might work. I've never seen him turn down a trade if the food he's getting is bigger."

We've had a can of Precious Pet in the cupboard ever since we took care of the Grubbs' cat last summer. I climbed on the counter and took it down.

Melissa and I stood by the can opener on the counter and looked at each other. "Should we really do this?" I asked.

"Does he deserve it?" she asked.

"Yo. Absolutely," I answered in my best Rocky imitation.

We had just added pickle relish and mayonnaise to the cat food when Dad walked into the kitchen. At the sight of him, we burst out laughing.

He stared at us. "You two will do great with boys. You really know how to inspire confidence."

We laughed harder, and he looked pleased. "What are you making?" he asked, leaning over to smell the bowl of cat food.

We were laughing so hard we couldn't talk.

Dad looked annoyed. "What's going on?" he asked.

I took big breaths. "Nothing," I lied. "Melissa just said that this tuna salad smelled like cat food."

"Oh. Well, you two are being sillier than usual. Assuming that's possible. When will the fudge be ready?"

"Soon. We'll bring everyone some," I said.

"Good. And we'll pass on the cat food."

As the door shut behind my father, Melissa grabbed me. "He knows!" she said. "He probably even knows what we were going to do!"

"No, he's just joking. That's how Robert jokes."

"Are you sure?" She still looked scared.

"I'm positive. If he knew, he sure wouldn't be joking."

"Maybe we shouldn't do it," she said.

"Maybe not," I agreed. "But since we made the stuff, I'm going to make a sandwich. I'll hide it in the refrigerator and bring it to school on Monday. Then we can decide if we'll do it or not."

"Good plan," she said. "Perfect. Get it? Purrrr-fect?"

After we hid the sandwich, we served the fudge. We ate enough ourselves to make our teeth itch.

◆ ◆ ◆

The next day, as we waited on the porch for Melissa's mother to come and pick her up because of the rain,

Melissa and I played the car game. To play this game, you say something terrible and then name two colors, such as, "I have to eat sixteen beetles, red and white." Then you watch the cars that come by. If you see a red car first, you have to eat the beetles, and if you see a white one first, you don't. No one really does the bad things, but it's fun to pretend, especially if no cars of either color come by for a long time.

If you play the car game on someone you don't like, you wish for the right color car to come along to make it true. We always wish bad things on Byron.

Today I said, "Mr. Garrett has to eat spider guts. Black and orange."

"No fair," Melissa answered.

She knew we'd see a black car before we saw an orange one because orange ones are the hardest to get.

"I don't care," I said. "I want him to lose. I hate him." I paused, but Melissa didn't speak. "Do you like him?" I asked.

"He's not bad."

"He was mean to my mother," I said.

"Really? When? What happened?"

I told her the story about Jake's note, and all through the story she said, "You're kidding!" She was more surprised about the note than she was about how Mr. Garrett treated my mom.

"But that's the rule," Melissa said. "He has to go by rules."

"Well, I don't think he should be able to boss my parents in their very own house."

She didn't answer.

"Melissa, that rule is so kids don't make fake excuses. Like saying they're at the dentist if they skipped school to play video games. I didn't skip. I was sick."

"I know," she said, but I could tell she didn't agree with me. She moves her lips in a certain way when she's mad.

"Well," I said, "I think he was wrong to tell my mom that." I was mad too, which seemed strange, because Melissa and I never argued. I could not believe that she was taking Mr. Garrett's side against my mom.

Just then Melissa's mother drove up and waved to us as she parked the car in front of our house. Melissa stood up and picked up her backpack. She was adjusting the straps, not looking at me, as she said, "Thanks for having me. I had a good time."

"I'm glad you came," I answered.

She got into the car and shut the door and she didn't look back as her mother drove away.

I watched the black car go around the corner.

Black car, I thought. Mr. Garrett eats spider guts. Good! Yum them in, Mr. Garrett.

5

I walked to school alone on Monday because Melissa had to go to the dentist. One of her fillings had fallen out. I hadn't talked to her since she left my house. We hadn't had an argument, really, but I didn't feel regular.

Melissa came in the door and quickly put her book bag away. Mr. Garrett had said that latecomers should disturb the class as little as possible, and he just kept on talking. I pretended to listen to him, but really I was noticing Melissa. She was wearing her tan dress with blue-plaid sleeves.

Melissa and I have a pact that whenever one of us walks behind the other one's chair, we tap the back of the chair two times. When she walked behind me I concentrated so I wouldn't miss it in case she tapped. I thought she would because we weren't fighting. Not really.

I was concentrating so hard that the taps almost

made me jump. They were two hard knocks, so loud that I thought Mr. Garrett might have heard them. Melissa thought so too, I could tell, because she looked embarrassed, but he just continued talking about decimals.

When lunchtime finally came and the lunch buyers were dismissed, Melissa looked over at me and then made a face at Byron's empty chair. Byron was down in the cafeteria, probably loading up on food already. He's always first in line.

Sometimes Sue Ann walks down with Melissa and me. Today I hoped she wouldn't because I couldn't talk about our plan in front of her. I was lucky. Sue Ann was still up at Mr. Garrett's desk talking to him when we left.

"Did you bring it?" Melissa asked, as soon as we got into the hall.

"Does a bus have wheels?" I answered.

"Do you think he'll really eat it?" she said.

"Do cats have fur?"

In the cafeteria, we bought our milk and went up to Byron's table. Melissa started to sit down on the bench across from him.

"Taken," he said in a mean voice, showing a mouthful of mashed potatoes.

"Don't lie, Byron," I answered, sitting down. "We're only here because our regular table's dirty," I lied.

He used his knife and spoon to make a barrier

between us and him. "Cross this line and you're dead meat," he said.

"Don't worry," I told him. "Everything over that line's invisible to us. Which is a relief."

He opened his mouth wide.

"Gag!" Melissa said.

"So much for invisible," Byron told me.

I pretended to ignore him and started to talk to Melissa about our social studies test. After a few minutes, I reached into my lunch box and said in a complaining voice, "I don't know why my mom makes me two sandwiches when I only eat one."

"Is it peanut butter?" Byron asked. "I'll take it."

"No, this one's different," I said.

"Why?" he wanted to know.

"How should I know, Byron? I guess she's used to people at Pause ordering different stuff, so she automatically makes different kinds of things. Probably my brother has two other kinds. But I don't want to give it away. I'll force some of it down."

"I'll trade you," he said.

"For what?"

"These carrot sticks," he said. "All of them."

"I wouldn't do it," Melissa said. "The sandwich is worth more."

"No one asked you, Prissa," Byron told her.

"Have you touched those carrot sticks?" I asked. "Any part of them? Even once?"

"Never! I hate carrots."

That was a complete lie. Byron doesn't hate any food too much to eat it.

"It's a deal," I said, handing him the plastic-wrapped sandwich.

"What kind is it?" he asked, as he took it.

"I don't know. Tuna, I think."

He unwrapped it and took a huge bite. "Yeah, it is," he said without swallowing. "But my dad's tuna salad is better than this. I hope your mom has a cook at that restaurant."

I was trying so hard not to laugh that I couldn't answer. Melissa's face was almost purple, as if she'd been holding her breath for a long time.

"I need to go to the bathroom," I said, standing up and grabbing my lunch box.

"I'll come too," Melissa said, and it was obvious that she was going to burst out laughing.

We walked away from the table quickly. As soon as I'd taken a few steps, Byron said, "Hey, Ellie!"

I turned to look back at him. "What?"

"I licked all those carrots. So one of us got tricked."

Melissa and I screamed with laughter and ran from the cafeteria.

◆ ◆ ◆

Sue Ann walked home with us after school. Her parents were going out, so she was going to spend the afternoon and evening at Melissa's. I was wishing that

Melissa and I were alone so we could talk about Byron. As it turned out, we talked about him anyway.

"I think I have to tell you, Ellie, that I don't think it was right what you did to Byron," Sue Ann said.

I looked at Melissa.

"I told her when we went on bathroom break," Melissa said.

I couldn't believe she'd told, but I couldn't say so with Sue Ann right there. Besides, Melissa didn't even look embarrassed. She was acting as if we were all three best friends, but we weren't.

"Anyway," Sue Ann went on, "you really do owe him an apology."

"Are you joking?" I asked, but I knew she wasn't.

"Not a bit," she answered, her mouth in a prissy line.

"What do *you* think?" I asked Melissa.

Melissa looked uncomfortable. "Well, I don't think you ought to apologize to him. I never would if I had done it."

"You *did* do it," I said. "We both did it."

"Well, right," Melissa answered. "I told you that, Sue Ann."

"Who first thought it up?" Sue Ann asked. She was staring at Melissa.

Melissa hesitated and then said, "Ellie."

"Who made the sandwich?" Sue Ann continued.

Melissa's voice was quiet. "Ellie," she said.

"And who gave it to him?" Sue Ann asked, like a lawyer on TV.

This time Melissa didn't answer and we all kept walking. I didn't know if I was madder at Sue Ann or Melissa. What made me even madder was that I'd been starting to feel bad about trading that sandwich to Byron. It had been funny all the time we were planning it. And when he first ate the sandwich, that was funny. But later in the afternoon, I looked over at him at his desk, and I felt not exactly sad and not exactly sorry, but just that it wasn't as funny as it had been. I'd hoped that when Melissa and I talked about it after school, it would get funny again. And now here was Sue Ann acting as if I'd done something really horrible. And worst of all, Melissa seemed to be agreeing with her. I knew I'd never admit that I felt at all bad about tricking Byron, since Sue Ann was trying to make me feel that way.

We were almost at my house. "Sue Ann," I said, "you're just mad because you didn't think it up. And even if you'd thought of it, you wouldn't have had the nerve to do it. Melissa and I did."

"No, *you* did," Sue Ann answered. "And if Byron or his parents find out, you're responsible. Like if they should sue."

"That is so dumb, it's sad," I said.

"What's sad," Sue Ann answered, "is that you're not even a little bit sorry for what you did to poor

Byron. At least Melissa sees that she shouldn't have encouraged you. Don't you, Melissa?"

Melissa looked miserable. "I don't know. We probably shouldn't have done it, Ellie," she said quietly.

"Well, maybe *you* can apologize to him," I said. "Sue Ann can tell you what to say." I turned and walked down my front walk and into my house.

◆　◆　◆

During the next few days at school, Melissa stayed around Sue Ann much more than she stayed around me. She didn't ignore me—she's not rude like that—but she acted as if Sue Ann was her friend and I wasn't.

I didn't say anything at home about Melissa and me having a fight because it wasn't a real fight, not something we'd have to make up. When I got into a fight with friends in first and second grade, one of us would always make up. We'd say, "Sorry," or else, "Do you want to be friends?" But in fifth, when people have a fight, they kind of let it fade away. If the other person acts friendly and you do too, you know that you're friends again. Melissa wasn't acting friendly now and neither was I.

But I wished things were back the way they were before the cat-food sandwich. I missed having Melissa to talk to. Besides, Bingo was going to Melissa's the weekend after next. If she and I didn't make up, I probably wouldn't get to play with him there.

During lunch on Tuesday and Wednesday, I sat at a different part of the table where most of the girls sit. Probably no one noticed that Melissa and I weren't sitting together. But I noticed.

◆　◆　◆

I helped Mom cook dinner on Thursday night. I made the salad. I could have made the whole meal because we were only having hot dogs and salad.

When Dad came to the table and saw the hot dogs, he said, "Has the Galloping Gourmet slowed down to a trot?"

"I don't need that, Robert," Mom said.

"I'm just teasing," Dad said.

"I know," Mom answered. "But I'm tired."

Jake was eating at Marvin's house. I think he likes Marvin's sister, Andrea, but he says he doesn't. Jake wouldn't admit it even if he did like her because he knows I'd make fun of him. Every time he comes back from Marvin's house I say, "How's Andrea the Pandrea?" and he always says, "She died."

As we finished dinner, I told my parents, "Melissa doesn't like me."

"Did you two have a disagreement?" Mom asked.

"A little. And now she's mad."

"Are you mad too?" my father wanted to know.

"I don't know," I said.

"I'm sure she still likes you," Mom said. "Just as you do her. But you tend to play with one person too much, and then when there's a disagreement, you're lonely till you make up. I've noticed that you've been mopey for the last few days."

"There's no one else to do things with," I said.

"Of course there is," Mom told me. "You can play with Sue Ann or Jenny or any number of people. Melissa's a good friend, but she's not the only person in the world."

"But you can't be best friends and tell secrets to just anyone, Mom. And Sue Ann thinks she's so precious perfect."

"That's not nice, Ellie," my mother said.

"Well, it's true," I answered.

I could feel that Mom was giving me an angry look. I kept my eyes on my plate.

Jake got home soon after I'd finished the dishes. When I asked how Andrea was, he said, "I don't know. I asked her, but she didn't hear me. She's gone deaf."

For Jake, that's pretty grown up.

6

awn and I were partners during art,
which means you share a drawing table,
and we were working on a project where you put
strips of tissue paper on a sheet of white paper, then
wet the tissue paper to make the colors run together.
It makes pretty water for aquarium backgrounds,
which is what everyone was making. Dawn had finished hers—she can do any art project in a few minutes—and she was drawing pictures of other kids in
the class. As soon as she draws a few lines, you can
tell who the person is.

Melissa shared a table with Sue Ann and I noticed
that they kept giggling about something. They were
acting pretty silly. It made me sad to remember that
Melissa and I used to have giggling fits too.

All of a sudden, without even thinking about it, as
I tore my blue paper into strips, I told Dawn, "Melissa
likes Joey in Ms. Bently's class."

"Joey the Frog?" Dawn asked. I could tell she was surprised.

"Yes. She told me."

"Why does she like Froggy?"

"He gives her cuts in tetherball," I said.

"Would you like someone for that?" Dawn asked. "I mean, *like* like?"

"I don't think so," I said. I was already beginning to be sorry I'd told her. "Help me with this corner part, Dawn," I said. "How wet should I make it?"

"Let me see it," she said, picking up the blue strips.

For the rest of art, we talked about the project. I wished Dawn would forget what I'd told her. What I really wished was that I hadn't told Dawn or anyone Melissa's secret.

During science, Mr. Garrett was talking about rivers and how they pick up rocks and soil and carry them along. As he turned his back to draw a cross section of a river on the board, Jenny whispered, "Ellie, Dawn has a note for you."

I looked over at Dawn. She held up a folded paper that she was going to hand to Maria, who would hand it to Jenny, who would hand it to me. I looked again at Mr. Garrett. He was adding boulders to one side of the river, and I was sure he'd draw some on the other side. I nodded to Dawn and held out my hand to Jenny.

I didn't see Mr. Garrett turn around, but I heard

him as he walked over to Maria, and I saw him as he reached out for the note.

During his first day of teaching in Room 101, he had told us that any notes that he intercepted would be read aloud to the class. He'd already done that with two other notes. I only hoped that Dawn had written something like, "What page do we have tonight for math?"

"This is addressed to Ellie from Dawn," Mr. Garrett said. "The content is something that I can't understand Dawn wasting her time on, since our science test is Monday and she'd benefit more by paying attention. She's drawn a picture of what looks like Melissa in line to play tetherball and Melissa is saying to a frog labeled Joey, 'If you give me cuts, I'll like you.'" He looked at Dawn. "Dawn, would you care to elaborate on this?"

She shook her head "No."

He looked at Maria. "You were passing it, Maria. Do you want to use your science time passing papers about a talking frog?"

"That's not a real frog," Maria said. "That's Joey Younkin in Ms. Bently's class."

"Regardless," Mr. Garrett said. "Questions about Joey Younkin *or* a real frog won't be on the test Monday. Is that clear, Ellie?" he said, turning to me.

I nodded my head. I didn't dare look over at Melissa. Byron was making frog sounds, "Ba-rump," and then he'd add a kissing sound after each croak. Mr. Garrett stared at him and the sounds stopped.

"Now," Mr. Garrett said, "let's return to our riverbed and see what we have."

I turned my eyes far enough to the right so I could just see Melissa. She had her science book open and propped up on her desk. Her face was almost in the book. Science seemed to last forever.

◆ ◆ ◆

Melissa didn't speak to me at lunchtime. I don't know if anyone else noticed. We were all at the girls' lunch table. Only Dawn, who had an appointment at the eye doctor, was missing. Everyone was saying things about the note except Melissa.

"Did she write it as a joke?" Jenny asked Melissa, who didn't answer.

"You *don't* like Frog, do you?" Sue Ann asked.

Melissa didn't answer her either. Finally, the girls stopped talking about the note. No one knew why Dawn had written it, but of course, I knew. And so did Melissa.

For the rest of the day, whenever Byron got a chance, he made frog croaks to Melissa. When Bruce started croaking too, Byron croaked louder and hopped around. His fat body, hopping down the aisle, was not a pretty sight. As he hopped by my desk, I stuck my foot out to trip him, but he jumped over it.

Just then, Mr. Garrett returned to the room so Byron had to walk back to his seat normally.

All through Byron's frog act Melissa ignored him, but I'm sure he knew that she saw what he was doing.

◆ ◆ ◆

My mom helped me dry dishes that night and I almost told her what had happened. In fact, I did, but I didn't tell her all of it.

"Something bad happened to Melissa today," I said.

"Really? What?" Mom asked.

"Well, she told this girl that she liked a certain boy, and the girl told Dawn, and Dawn drew a note about it. Mr. Garrett got the note and read it out loud, so now, everyone knows that Melissa likes the Frog."

"The frog?"

"We call him that because he's little and kind of looks like a frog."

"Does he know people call him that?"

"Well, sure, Mom. Like, if I'd say, 'Frog, here's a Twinkie,' he'd know to take it."

"But would you say that?"

"No, because I never have Twinkies. And if I did, I wouldn't give them to Frog."

"But, I mean, would you call him that to his face?"

"Yes. Everyone does. It's like his name."

"Well, I don't think that's kind, Ellie. I'd rather you didn't call him that. And I'm sure he'd rather it too."

"But, Mom, what about Melissa?"

"What about her?"

"I was telling you about the note saying she liked Frog. *That's* the bad part, not Frog's name."

Mom thought about it as she dried a plate. "Are you sure she didn't want people to know?"

"Yes! She made the girl promise not to tell. But the girl told Dawn and then Dawn drew it."

"That's a shame. Did Dawn and the girl apologize?"

I was quiet for a minute. "No. Dawn went to the eye doctor. Besides, she didn't mean for anyone to see the note. Just the girl who had told."

"Did the other girl apologize?"

"No," I said. I kept looking at the pan that I was drying.

"She should," my mother said. "And then Melissa needs to be careful who she tells her secrets to."

"Do you think she should still tell them to that girl? If the girl apologizes?"

"I don't know," Mom said, as she rinsed out the sponge. "I probably wouldn't. Would you?"

I didn't answer and Mom didn't ask me again.

"Be sure to wipe off the counter," she said as she left the kitchen.

"I will," I said.

I was sure Melissa wouldn't be friends with me again. Even my own mother wouldn't tell that girl secrets anymore. My mother just didn't know that that girl was me. I knew it though.

7

On Friday after school, I said to Mom, "I'm bored. I can't think of anything to do."

"Well, I certainly can, miss," she said. "Tomorrow we're going to get this house spotless. It's fine with me if you want to start today."

"I don't mean work stuff, Mom. You know what I mean."

"Do you want to invite Melissa over?" she asked.

"She doesn't like me."

"You two haven't made up? It's been a week. Why don't you invite her over and that will take care of it."

Mom didn't know that things between Melissa and me had gotten worse. All week Byron kept teasing Melissa about liking Frog. Every time he did it, it reminded me that he'd never know if I hadn't told. I'm sure it reminded Melissa too. She spoke to me, but only for real stuff that she had to say. She didn't talk to me for fun.

"I can't call her," I told Mom. "She's mad, and I know it."

"Then call someone else. What about Sue Ann?"

"I might," I said, not meaning it.

I went into the kitchen and made myself a sandwich and thought about it. Maybe the best way for me to try to make up with Melissa was to get to be friends with Sue Ann. Sue Ann was acting regular to me. Besides, she'd be someone to talk to, and we might even have fun. It wouldn't hurt to call.

Her mother answered the phone. "How nice to hear from you," she said when I told her my name. I don't know why the same polite things that make me feel good when Sue Ann's mother says them can make me sick when Sue Ann says them.

"Hi, Ellie," Sue Ann said, after a minute. "How are you?"

"Fine," I said. "Can you come over for a while?"

"I'd love to, but I'm going to spend the night with Melissa, and I still have things to do before I go. I want to take a few treats to Bingo. He's at Melissa's this weekend."

"Yes, I know."

"So I need to get those things together, and then my mother wants to French-braid my hair, and you know how long that takes."

"Yes, I know," I said again.

"Maybe I can come over a different time."

"Okay. See you later."

"Bye, Ellie. Oh, and thanks for calling."

My mother was still reading in the living room.

"Sue Ann can't come," I told her. "I called her."

"Oh. Well, you could try Jenny, though to tell you the truth I was thinking of taking you and Jake to see that horse movie tonight."

We ate dinner early and got ready for the movie. Dad went with us, and not only was the movie wonderful, but we went out for ice cream afterwards. Even Jake acted human, so it was fun.

◆ ◆ ◆

On Monday I couldn't find my math homework. I knew I'd put it either in my math book or in my social studies book, but I looked through every page and couldn't find it. Mr. Garrett and the class waited to correct as I searched.

"I can't find it," I said. "I did it. I did it on Friday, but it's not here. Maybe I dropped it on the way to school."

Jenny was nodding, but Mr. Garrett didn't even look at her. "That's one recess then," he said.

I'd never missed having a homework assignment as long as I'd been in school, and it made me mad that I had to stay in just as if I hadn't done the paper.

Ms. Simpson never made us miss recess. She said she thought it was important for us to get out, and besides she believed us when we said we had done our homework. Mr. Garrett says it's not that he doesn't believe us, but that it's a matter of responsibility.

I could see everyone outside playing while I worked on the boards during recess. Byron came to the window and made a face at me and ran away. Then Jenny came up to wave.

She stood there smiling as I wrote, "Hi, Jenny," on the board. Then as she watched, I drew a giant heart and wrote inside it, "Ellie Brader Hates Mr. G."

Jenny laughed and then pointed out toward the swings. When I came to the window to look, I saw Scott hanging upside down from the top of the swing-set bar and Ms. Rigby rushing over to make him come down.

Behind me, I heard the sound of metal rubbing on metal. I turned to look and saw Mr. Garrett opening his desk drawer. He took out a paper. He started toward the door, but he stopped at the board to read what I'd written. He stared at the heart for a long time. Then he said, "I'm sorry you feel that way," and left the room.

I sat down at the first desk. My face felt so hot I thought it would burn up. I had been positive that Mr. Garrett was out on the playground. Now he'd hate me forever, and I couldn't blame him. And the truth was, I didn't hate him. I didn't like him. I liked Ms. Simpson a lot and wished like anything that she was still our teacher, but I didn't actually *hate* Mr. Garrett.

I was mad at him for making me stay in, and I was showing off to make Jenny laugh.

I got up from the desk and erased everything on the board except the homework assignments. I rubbed the board with the sponge side of the eraser and then with the chamois side, the way Mr. Garrett had told us to do. When the class came back, I was waiting in my seat with my science book out.

After lunch, Mr. Garrett announced that Beverly's mother had told him that Beverly would be missing some school because of an operation on her knee. He said that Bingo's care for the week would have to go to the next person after Beverly, which was me.

"Please bring a note from your parents, Ellie, to show that they're agreeable to having the rabbit for this coming weekend. I'd imagine that they'll say yes, since I see from this list that you've had him at home before."

I nodded.

"As for today," he continued, "you can give him more pellets and water. Then tomorrow, if you want to bring some cabbage or whatever, you may."

I nodded again.

"You may feed him while I pass out these booklets."

I went to Bingo's cage and petted him through the wire. Then I reached in and petted him as I poured the rabbit pellets into his dish. Since his water bottle was full, I didn't have to add any water.

As I shut his cage door, Bingo did his cutest thing. He yawned. When he yawned, his top and bottom teeth showed—otherwise you never saw them—and they looked so sweet against his dark fur and pink tongue.

◆ ◆ ◆

Jake was home when I got there.

"I get Bingo this weekend," I said.

"Good," Jake said. "I didn't know it was so soon."

"It's really Beverly's turn but she has to have an operation on her knee."

"We should try to teach him some tricks this time. He was too young before, but I bet he could learn now. Probably no one's tried."

"Like what?" I asked.

"Can he sit up on his back legs? Does he ever?"

"Yes."

"We could train him to do that when we say a certain thing."

"Okay," I said. "We'll work with him. But I'm the boss because I'm really in charge of him."

"Maybe," Jake said.

I wondered if he was trying to start a fight.

Mom came into the kitchen carrying a grocery bag.

"What's that?" Jake asked.

"It's your mother," Mom said. "Aren't you going to say hello?"

"Hello," Jake said. "What's in the bag? Something for me?"

"No. For your father. Shirts on sale. Are you kids hungry?"

"Yes," Jake said, opening the refrigerator.

"I get Bingo this weekend," I said. "And I get to take care of him during the week."

"How nice," Mom said.

"I know. But I need a note. One by you, not by Jake."

Mom smiled. "You're right. I'd hate to think what he would write about a rabbit."

"Do we have some vegetables I can take for Bingo to eat tomorrow?"

"I'm sure we do. Check while I put these away."

◆　◆　◆

After dinner Jenny called me up about our science homework assignment. I hadn't done it yet. When I went to my room for the book, I saw my math paper sitting on the table. I'd been positive that I'd put it into my math book.

"Let me turn to that page," I told Jenny. "You know my math paper? It's here on my table. I didn't put it in my book."

"At least you don't have to do it again," she said.

"Yes. But do you know what happened today? When you were at recess and I wrote that I hated Mr.

Garrett on the board, he came back in the room and saw it."

"Oh, no! Maybe he didn't read it."

"He did," I said. "He read it and said, 'I'm sorry you feel that way.'"

"Oh, no," she said again. "Was he mad?"

I thought about it. "No, not really. He sounded kind of sad. And I didn't say Sorry, or anything. I didn't talk."

"I wouldn't have either."

"He probably hates me now."

"He let you take care of Bingo," she said.

"Well, he had to. I was next on the list."

"I guess so," she said.

"I've got the page now," I said. "I'll read you the chart and then you can memorize it."

"But I need to write it down. How could I have left my dumb book?"

"I know," I said. "Let's start with the planets."

"Ready," Jenny said.

◆ ◆ ◆

It was almost seven o'clock when I decided to call Melissa. I missed her a lot and I wanted to tell her about writing on the board. I thought I'd feel better if I told her. Jenny was a good friend, especially for fun times. But I needed Melissa, my best friend, to make me feel better about what I'd done. Sometimes my family can help, but I sure wasn't going to admit to my family what I'd done. I *knew* I wouldn't feel better if I told them.

I also wanted to tell Melissa that I was sorry I hadn't kept her secret. As I dialed her number, I hoped she was as ready to make up as I was.

Melissa's younger sister, June, answered the phone.

"This is Ellie. Is Melissa there?" I asked.

"Maybe yes, maybe no, maybe rain, maybe snow," June answered. She is a true pain.

"June, get your sister," I said, my voice meaner. I didn't call her June Bug, which is what Melissa calls her, because I was afraid she'd hang up. She's done that before.

"What's the magic word?" June asked.

Kill, I thought. "Please," I said.

"She's not here."

"Are you lying?"

"No. She went to make up a piano lesson. But she wouldn't talk to you anyway. She can't stand you."

"You *are* lying now," I said, afraid that what she was saying was true.

"I am not," she said in her brattiest voice. "She says you have a mouth problem."

I didn't answer for a moment. Then I said calmly, "June, listen. When Melissa gets home, will you tell her to call me? Please?"

"Maybe yes, maybe no, maybe—"

"June, listen. If you're not old enough to tell her to call, let me talk to your mother."

"I'll tell her. But maybe she won't."

I stayed up a little past my bedtime but the phone didn't ring. Well, it rang, but it wasn't for me.

8

*T*he next day I brought green cabbage and half a cucumber to school for Bingo and watched him eat them. Before Bingo ate, he licked his paws so he looked as if he was washing his hands for dinner. The bottoms of his paws weren't black like his body but more brownish, like his back and tail. When his ears stuck straight up with the light from the windows behind them, I could see the pattern of veins in his ears.

Melissa hadn't spoken to me during the morning. At lunch, I thought about asking Melissa if June had given her my message, but I couldn't quite decide to do it. All the girls at the table were discussing the film we were going to see during health class. In our school, when boys and girls are in fifth grade, they see films about how men and women develop. The boys see the men film and the girls see the women one. I was anxious to see it.

After gym, Ms. Rankin asked us to line up, boys and girls separately, and file into two health rooms. Everyone was giggling and acting silly. Byron ran over and got in the girls' line, as if he wanted to see the girls' film, and a few boys whistled.

"You look as though you belong there, Byron," Bruce said. "You fit in that line."

Byron walked back to the boys' line and made a fist at Bruce as he passed him.

"Say that to my face," Byron said, holding up his fist.

"You fit in that line," Bruce said to Byron's face.

"Yeah," Byron said, "you know I can't do anything about it here." He walked to the end of the boys' line.

We sat down at the desks in the health room and Ms. Rankin pulled down the green window shades that block out the light during a film.

"Girls," she said, "I'm sure that each of you is mature enough to see and enjoy this film. I say 'enjoy' because most people enjoy learning about themselves. The film is about you, what will happen to your bodies, what's already happening to your bodies. We'll have time for questions afterwards."

Some of the film was a cartoon that showed the inside of a woman and what changes were happening to her body each month. The rest of the film had real people in it, girls about our age. The movie was good and not long, about twenty minutes. When it ended,

Ms. Rankin said, "Would anyone care to see it again?"

We all raised our hands and she rewound it and started it over. It was better the second time. I could get the parts that I didn't understand, the parts I'd missed because I was thinking about what I'd seen a few minutes earlier.

Ms. Rankin told us to write down questions but not to sign our names, so people wouldn't know who asked what. But when Ms. Rankin read, "When is a girl old enough to wear a bra if she doesn't have any breasts?" we all knew who'd written it. It was written on yellow lined paper, and Brenda is the only one who uses that kind. Besides, Brenda fits the description of the girl.

Ms. Rankin said it was understandable that when we saw our friends developing and starting to wear bras, we might want to too. She said the question-writer's time was coming any day. I thought Ms. Rankin was nice about it. I also thought that if Brenda's time was coming soon, then mine was too.

The boys were already back in Room 101 when we arrived. Shannon said their film must have been short because nothing happens to them.

"Yes, it does," Sue Ann told her. "Their voices change and they grow hair."

"So?" Shannon said. "How long can you sit and watch hair grow?"

"Hi, girlies," Byron said, as we walked past his desk. "We got popcorn at our movie."

"You need it, Byron," Dawn said, sitting down.

◆ ◆ ◆

It was my turn to wash dishes that night.

"We saw this film in health today," I told my parents, after Jake had left the table when he finished eating. "The one you got the note from school about."

"How was it?" Dad asked.

"Good. We saw it twice. Then we asked questions. I think maybe I'm old enough to get a bra."

"Well," my mother said, "maybe so. But I don't think you're quite ready yet."

"Why?" I asked.

"Well," she said again, "it's not a matter of age, really. Do many of the fifth-grade girls have bras?"

"Tons," I told her.

She looked at me.

"Maybe not tons, but some."

"We can think about it," she said. "I think it would be rushing it a little at this point. But we can think about it."

"Do you think it's rushing it?" I asked Dad.

"I do," he said. "And it doesn't matter how many girls in fifth grade have bras. It's not something to vote on, like the majority rules."

"But that's somewhat of a factor," Mom told him. "It is, Robert."

"It wasn't when I was in school," he said. "I was in ninth grade before I got a bra."

"Dad, you're silly," I said, but I laughed.

Mom didn't laugh. She thinks Dad sometimes says inappropriate things, and I knew that joke was one of them. She acts like some of Dad's funniest jokes are inappropriate, but I can tell she still thinks they're funny.

◆ ◆ ◆

On Thursday morning, Sue Ann wasn't at school. When Mr. Garrett called her name, Melissa spoke. "Sue Ann is absent because she has chicken pox," she said. "She won't be back until sometime next week."

Breaks my heart, I thought. Then immediately I felt bad because I remembered that Sue Ann had sent me a get-well card when I had the chicken pox. The card had two sticks of chewing gum inside. I guess she chewed the other three.

Mr. Garrett made some people trade seats. A few moves were to stop talkers—he called those "preventive maintenance"—but some were for other reasons. I was moved up to Allison's seat, right by Mr. Garrett's desk, because now that her glasses finally came, she gets headaches from being that close to the board.

On Thursday we worked on standardized tests. Every fifth grade in the country takes the same ones. There are a lot of rules. You can only use certain pencils and the booklets can't be opened until a certain moment. The main thing is that people aren't supposed to leave the room while the test is going on. Teachers put a card on the outside of the door that says we're testing so no one will bother us.

Half way through the spelling section Scott came up and asked Mr. Garrett if he could leave and go to the bathroom.

"Can it wait, Scott?" Mr. Garrett asked. "This test will be over in ten minutes."

"Okay," Scott said, and returned to his desk.

When the recess bell rang, Jenny helped me take Bingo out of his cage. Jenny had brought some raw spinach leaves for him, and we were going to give them to him for his recess snack. I looked around for Melissa, thinking maybe she'd want to help with Bingo too, but she was busy talking with Dawn and Maria.

Jenny and I hopped Bingo by walking around the playground with him, but this was one of those days when he wanted to hang around and bite people's shoelaces. I followed him as he hopped up to Wallace and nibbled his sneakers. Wallace laughed and looked at me. "I guess he likes dirt," he said.

"I guess so," I answered. Then I wondered if it

sounded like I was saying that I thought Wallace's shoes were dirty. They were, but I didn't want to say so.

After recess, I put Bingo back in his cage and then sat down at my desk.

"We will now resume the final portion of the spelling test," Mr. Garrett said. "You're allowed ten minutes and I'll set the timer as soon as you open your booklets. Open your booklets now."

The class was quiet except for the occasional sound of someone moving in a chair. No one even got up to sharpen a pencil. Mr. Garrett had made sure that everyone began the test with two sharp pencils so we wouldn't have to use up any of our test time.

I was surprised when Scott walked up to Mr. Garrett's desk again.

"Yes?" Mr. Garrett asked.

"Mr. Garrett," Scott said, looking embarrassed, "I have to go to the bathroom."

"Didn't you go during recess?" Mr. Garrett asked.

"I forgot. I was playing basketball."

"Well, you couldn't have to go that badly then. There's four minutes left in this test. You can wait that long."

Scott turned and walked back to his seat.

He was back at his desk for less than a minute. I didn't have time to finish a question before he returned to the front of the room. This time he stood at the side of Mr. Garrett's desk, closer to the door. He said, "Mr. Garrett!" and his voice sounded desperate.

"Go ahead, Scott. You may leave," Mr. Garrett said quickly, but it was too late.

A puddle grew on the floor around Scott's sneakers. He turned toward the door, but his foot slipped in the puddle and he almost fell. He caught himself and ran from the room. I saw that he was starting to cry.

Mr. Garrett sat there and we pretended to keep working on our tests. At least, I pretended. Maybe everyone else was really working.

Soon Mr. Garrett said, "Time. Close your booklets. I will be gone for a few minutes. Dawn, collect the booklets, then you all may read your library books or work on tonight's homework."

As soon as the door shut behind him, we all started talking.

"Scott was crying," Maria said. "I could tell."

"Do you think he'll come back today?" Shannon asked.

"I sure wouldn't," Joan said.

"Maybe he'll be back with diapers on," Byron said.

"Oh, shut up," Melissa told him.

"Kiss a frog!" Byron yelled.

We were still talking when Mr. Garrett returned. No one had taken out a library book.

Mr. Garrett sat down slowly, which made him look older than usual. "I want your undivided attention," he said, and everyone was silent. "I'm sure you saw what happened, and if you didn't, your classmates informed you while I was gone. Scott had an accident. Because I made a mistake. Scott's father will be bringing some other clothes, but whether Scott will have the courage to return to class today, I don't know. He will return, however, either today or tomorrow. At that time I ask for your help for him. I ask you not to tease him or make fun of him because of an accident that was my fault and not his." He paused for a moment. "Simply use good sense and kindness. Try to learn from my mistake." He looked out the window, then back to us. "Take out your math books and turn to the Practice for Skill section."

We were doing the multiple choice part when I heard the door knob turn. The door opened slowly and Scott stepped inside. I could tell that he'd been crying and also that he'd combed his hair.

Scott walked to his desk, looking down at the floor. Mr. Garrett said, "We're on page two eighty-three. We're beginning the multiple choice."

Scott took his math book out, opened it, and began to work.

The whole class stayed quiet until lunchtime. Walking down the hall to the cafeteria, I saw Scott with Wallace and Randy. I knew those two boys would be nice to him. Scott was acting regular, talking about some lay-up shot that he'd seen on television. I could tell he was going to be okay.

◆   ◆   ◆

My dog was waiting outside for me when I got home from school. He's always so happy to see me that he jumps from side to side on his back legs as though he's dancing.

"Prance and dance, Willie," I said, which makes him do it harder. I decided to work on Willie's training program for a while.

I was training Willie in the backyard, and Mom was sitting in the lawn chair, resting, when Jake got home. Jake brought his bike tire out to the yard to work on it, and right away he started being a pain.

"Tomorrow," Jake said, "I'm going to train Willie to jump through a ring of fire."

"You know you're lying, you cow," I answered.

"Ellie, just ignore him," Mom said.

"Well, I don't like him acting as if he's going to hurt Willie."

"Hey," Jake said, "if Willie is fast, he won't get hurt."

"That's sufficient, Jake," Mom said. "I mean it."

Jake went back to working on his bike tire, singing, "I jumped through a burning ring of fire."

"I'm going to send you into the house if you don't stop," Mom told him.

He stopped singing and continued to fix his bike tire.

◆ ◆ ◆

Mom let me cook dinner. She stayed in the kitchen with me cleaning the bottoms of pans.

"I want to be in here," she said, "but I want to be busy or I'll tell you how to do it too much."

Even Mom knows that she lectures. She loves to give advice whether you want it or not.

At dinner everyone in the family, even Jake, said my chili was good.

"Your turn tomorrow night," Mom said to Jake, helping herself to more chili.

"Mr. Garrett made Scott wet his pants today," I said.

"That sounds like a medical miracle," Dad answered.

"It wasn't funny," I said. "Scott cried." I told them what had happened.

"Garrett probably thought it was funny," Jake said.

I looked at him and could tell he wasn't joking.

"No," I told him. "He's not like that."

"Then what's he like?" Jake asked.

I thought for a moment. "I don't know. But not like that."

"Did that ever happen to you, Dad?" Jake asked, and he was smiling. "When you were in school?"

"No," Dad said. "That didn't happen to me till I was in the Army."

"Robert," Mom said.

"Luckily no one could tell because I was wearing camouflage. That was a lifesaver."

"Please pass the salad," Mom told Dad, though she still had a little on her plate.

9

ake went to school early on Friday for a photography club meeting, and Dad dropped him off. Mom and I ate breakfast together.

"So Bingo arrives today, huh?" Mom asked, as she buttered her toast.

"Yep. You'll think he's bigger than last time, I'll bet."

"Probably. I was thinking you might want to invite Melissa to spend the night, since you'll have Bingo here. I know she'd enjoy seeing him."

I didn't answer.

"Isn't it time you actively worked on making up?" Mom asked.

"I don't know. She's friends with Sue Ann now."

"Well, you're friends with other people too, and that's not an issue."

"I know."

Neither one of us said anything for a while. I made a line of raisins around the rim of my cereal bowl.

"Mom, remember when I told you that a girl told Melissa's secret about liking Frog?"

"Yes."

"Well, I'm the one who did it."

She looked at me for a moment. (It was a long moment.) "Why did you tell?" she asked.

"I don't know. Melissa wasn't being friends with me, and I was mad, and I just said it."

"And you didn't apologize?"

"No."

"I think you should. For that, you should."

"Maybe so. I'll think about it more."

"Good," Mom said. "More juice?"

"Yes, please. Sometimes I think I'm jealous. I mean when Melissa acts like she likes Sue Ann best."

"Of course you are."

"I am?"

"Probably," Mom said. "It sounds like it."

"I wish I wouldn't be."

"It's a normal feeling. For everyone, including adults."

"Are you ever jealous?"

"Sometimes. Everyone is. Adults just don't admit it as much. You'll see what I mean when you're older."

I knew that meant Mom was finished talking about it unless I said something else. When she says, "You'll see when you're older," that's usually her last thing.

We both stood up and cleared off the table.

◆ ◆ ◆

School passed slowly because I was anxious for it to end so I could take Bingo home. After recess, Mr. Garrett showed us a shoe box with its lid taped shut. A slot had been cut in the center of the lid.

"This is the box we will use for the drawing to see who keeps Bingo," he said. "When you bring your note from home, you'll be allowed to write your name on one of these special tickets, then put the ticket in the box. We'll have the drawing in exactly two weeks, so you have that long to get your permission note in to me. At two o'clock on the drawing date, your name must be in the box or else you can't be included. Any questions?"

"What if someone puts in two tickets?" Byron asked. "Or more?"

"Since I have the tickets, no one will. But I hope that was just a theoretical question. Does anyone know the definition of the word *theoretical*?"

No one raised a hand.

"All right," Mr. Garrett said. "Let's begin our spelling assignment. At the end of the paper, I'd like each of you to write down what you find in the dictionary when you look up the word *theoretical*. I'd also like you to write a sentence using the word correctly. And Dawn, if you have any free time today, perhaps you could draw some appropriate decorations on our rabbit raffle box. Unfortunately, my artistic skills are sadly lacking. Mark, you can be her assistant."

A few kids giggled because everyone knew that Mark and Dawn liked each other. Mr. Garrett was smiling as if he knew too, but I was sure he couldn't have known.

"Is there a problem, Wallace?" Mr. Garrett said to Wallace, who was still laughing.

"No. But Mark's not good in art."

"I assumed he was hanging around Dawn on the playground so he could improve in it," Mr. Garrett answered, and everyone laughed. "Consider this a golden opportunity, Mark," he added, smiling.

So I guess Mr. Garrett did know, but I don't know who told him.

Dawn decorated the box with a picture of Bingo standing in a garden eating flowers. A ladybug sat on one of his ears, and a yellow butterfly rested on his tail. There was a sign in the garden that said, "Welcome home, Bingo." Dawn really can draw.

As I carried Bingo's cage out of the classroom after school, I wondered which way Melissa would walk home. When we were friends, she used to walk with me and then turn off at her street. It added two blocks to her trip, but we got to talk on the way home. Ever since we'd had our fight, she'd gone the short way, a way that takes her to her house faster. As soon as we left school, Melissa walked ahead. I hoped maybe she'd want to see Bingo so much that she'd come my way today, but I saw her turn off toward the shortcut. I almost called out to her and asked her to walk with me, thinking that maybe then I could apologize, but I didn't. I watched her as she disappeared down the street, her blue blouse becoming a tiny dot.

Jake and Mom were waiting at home when I arrived.

"You *are* bigger," Mom said to Bingo. "Come out of that cage."

I took him out and let him hop around the kitchen. Mom and Jake petted him and said how cute he was. Mom put a bowl of water down for him but he wasn't thirsty.

Jake and I sat on the floor with our backs against the kitchen cabinets and watched Bingo investigate each table leg.

"Boy, I hope I win him," I said.

"Me too," Jake answered.

◆ ◆ ◆

Jenny called on Saturday morning to ask if she could come over and play with Bingo.

"Are you and Jake still going to train him to do tricks?" she asked.

"I want to," I said. "Jake's over at Marvin's. Do you want to help me?"

"Sure," she said. "I'll come as soon as I clean my room. Or right away, if my mom forgets to tell me to clean up."

I let Bingo play in the backyard while I waited for Jenny. He hopped around the backyard, exploring every bush and plant. He seemed to like it best under the lilac bush, since that's where he ended up each time after circling the yard.

When Jenny arrived, Bingo was under the bush and I was reading.

"Hi," Jenny said, coming through the back gate. "I brought my autograph book."

"Let's see it," I said, holding out my hand.

She handed the red book to me. It had the word *Autographs* printed on its front cover in gold.

"I got it from my aunt last week. In the mail. Because Mom told her about my good grades."

"I like it," I told her. "Has anyone signed it?"

"No. I thought you and Bingo could be the first. Maybe we could put his paw print in it."

"Good idea. I don't have an ink pad, though. What else can we use?"

Jenny thought for a moment. "How about mud?" she asked, looking at a mud puddle near the corner of the yard.

"Okay. But we'll try it on regular paper first," I said. "We don't want to mess the book up."

"Right. Shall I watch Bingo while you get paper?"

"Yes. And I'll bring us something to eat."

I decided to make our snack fancy so I took the green tray out of the cupboard. I put two white plates on the tray, then cut up two oranges. On each plate, I made a circle of orange sections and then put a cherry in the center of each circle. The oranges looked a little bit like flowers. I poured lemonade into tall glasses, and I even added two cherries. The drinks looked beautiful, like something you'd get at a fancy restaurant. Balancing the tray with both hands, I picked up a few sheets of notebook paper between my fingers.

"I'll help you," Jenny said, when she saw the tray. "I've got the paper. Oh, how pretty."

"Thanks," I said, letting the paper go and resting the tray on the yard table. "I didn't bring Bingo anything else because he's got a ton of snacks out here."

Jenny and I sat down to eat and watch Bingo play. Every time he peeked out from under the lilac bush, he'd hop up to us and sniff our sneakers and nibble our shoelaces.

"Too bad we can't make him some tiny tennis shoes," Jenny said.

"Yes, with decorated laces."

"And he could wear a matching one around his head," Jenny added.

After we finished our snack, we picked Bingo up to practice making paw prints. Jenny held the paper in her lap on the tray and I pressed Bingo's front paw into the mud. The first two prints were too messy. No one would have known that they were paw prints. But on the third try, some of the extra mud was gone, and the print was clear.

"Open the book," I said. "We'll do it before his foot dries."

She opened the autograph book to the section labeled "Special Friends." She held the book steady on the tray, and I pressed Bingo's paw against the page. It looked great.

"Let's wash his foot off," I said.

"Okay. And then I want to write his name under his print."

We rinsed Bingo's paw under warm water and I dried it on an old towel. In a moment he was hopping back to the lilac bush.

"Now you sign it too," Jenny said, holding out the book.

I thought for a while before I wrote. I didn't want to write a "Roses are red" autograph because everyone writes those. Instead, I wrote the one that says, "All the gold at the rainbow's end, can't compare with a good, true friend. Stay sweet. Your friend, Ellie."

Jenny read it when I gave it back to her. "Thanks," she said. "Should I print or write Bingo's name?"

"Print. It'll look more real."

"Un-huh," she agreed, printing the rabbit's name next to the paw print.

Jenny and I played Monopoly until lunch time,

made some sandwiches, and played some more. By the time she had to go home, she'd won most of the money and had tons of property.

"Your mistake was not buying those railroads," she said, as she got her things together to leave.

I hate it when people who just beat me at something tell me what my mistake was. I almost told Jenny how that bugs me, but I changed my mind. What if she'd gotten mad? Melissa already didn't like me. If I kept making people mad, I soon wouldn't have any friends at all.

After Jenny left, I stayed out in the yard with Bingo and read. When I'd finished three more chapters and almost knew the secret of the cave, Jake came into the yard. He sat in the other lawn chair.

I put my book down. "Do you want to teach Bingo tricks?" I asked.

Jake thought about it for a minute. "Have you taught him any yet?"

"No. Jenny came over but we didn't do that. I waited for you."

"Okay. Where is he?"

"Under the lilac bush," I said.

"Will he come out when you call him?"

"No. Not really. Shall we teach him that first?"

"Yes. I'll get cabbage to reward him," Jake said.

"Okay."

When Jake got back with the cabbage, he said that

I should call Bingo's name over and over. Just as soon as the rabbit came out from under the bush, Jake would give him a cabbage treat. The next time, Bingo would have to hop all the way over to the person calling him to get a treat.

"That'll be good," I said. "You get by the bush with the cabbage."

Jake crouched down by the bush with the cabbage ready.

"Bingo, Bingo," I called. "Bingo, come here. Come on, Bingo." Nothing happened.

"Are you sure he's under here?" Jake asked.

"Yes," I said. "He doesn't know his name that well." I called louder. "Bingo, come out."

"Let me check," Jake said, and he knelt down and peered under the bush.

"He's not here, Ellie," Jake said, and then he added, "Oh, no."

"What is it?" I asked, coming to the bush. "What, Jake?" Suddenly I felt scared.

"I think he's sick," Jake said. "Ellie, call Mom and Dad."

"How sick? How can you tell?" I knelt down beside my brother and ducked my head under the bottom of the bush.

There, on the brown leaves, Bingo lay on his side. He was perfectly still. His eyes were open but he wasn't looking at anything.

"Jake, is he dead?" I whispered.

"I think so," Jake said. "I'll get Dad. You come too."

"No. I'll stay by him," I said.

Jake stood up and ran toward the back door.

"Bingo?" I said and I touched his soft side fur. "Bingo?" The rabbit didn't move.

"Let me see, Ellie," my dad said, kneeling beside me.

After looking at Bingo for a moment, he said, "Honey, this rabbit isn't alive."

"I know," I said, starting to cry. I crawled out from under the bush and stood up.

My mother was there beside my brother and she reached out and put her arms around me. "Let's go in the house," she said. "We'll find something to wrap him up in."

"Are we going to bury him?" Jake asked.

"Yes," she said. "Do you want to come with us?"

"I'll help Dad," he said, kneeling down beside the bush.

I gave up trying not to cry. Tears dripped down my face, and I just wiped them away with my hand.

Mom and I got a shoe box and an old white towel with pink flowers on it. We took them both out into the yard where Dad and Jake were waiting and Dad carefully wrapped the towel around Bingo. When he folded the material over the rabbit's face and ears, Jake started biting his lip as though he was trying not to cry. Dad held the rabbit while Mom got the shovel from the garage.

"I think we should put him in the flower garden," Mom said. "What do you think?" she asked Jake and me.

We both nodded.

Mom dug a few shovelfuls of dirt in the soft ground.

"I'll do it now," Dad said. He handed the rabbit's wrapped body to Mom and dug for a while, then stopped.

"Is it deep enough?" Jake asked.

"No," my father said. "We want it deep for dogs." He dug some more then finally said, "Let's bury him now."

Mom put Bingo into the shoe box and carefully closed the lid, making sure to tuck all the towel edges into the box.

"Shall I put him in the ground?" Mom asked us.

"Do you want me to do it, Joyce?" Dad asked her.

"No." She bent down and lowered the box into the hole.

Dad stood there with the shovel for a moment. His face looked sad. "Kids," he said, "I'm sorry this happened. But this rabbit had a very good life."

Dad started shoveling dirt into the hole. He did it carefully at first, dropping small amounts of dirt onto the box, but as the hole filled up, he shoveled more, adding large scoops of dirt until the hole was gone.

While Dad packed down the dirt, Mom brought a flowerpot of ferns and set it on top of the grave.

I was crying hard and I could hear Jake sniffing. As I looked at Bingo's grave, I thought of the garden that Dawn had drawn on the box at school. I remembered that in Dawn's picture, Bingo was playing and the sign said, "Welcome home, Bingo." I looked at the new hill of dirt in our garden. Then I closed my eyes tight and without saying it out loud, I told Bingo good-bye.

10

On Sunday morning, Mom told me she was going to call Mr. Garrett and let him know about Bingo.

"He'll blame me," I said. "Everyone will. I hope Jenny doesn't come over today. I don't want anyone to know."

Mom closed the telephone book and sat down.

"I know how you feel, Ellie, but I'm sure you're wrong. It wasn't your fault. It's not as though Bingo got hit by a car or something because you weren't watching him. Dad called the vet last night. The vet said that rabbits and birds can die quite suddenly. Often no one knows why. That's one reason why dogs and cats are probably better pets."

I didn't answer.

"I'm going to call him now," Mom said. "Okay?"

"Okay," I answered, but I didn't mean it.

I could hear Mom's half of the conversation. She

told Mr. Garrett what had happened and that we had buried Bingo. Then she was quiet while he talked and finally she said, "Yes, I agree. That's a good idea. Yes, yes, I will."

She hung up the phone and said, "Mr. Garrett suggested that I drop you off at school tomorrow right when classes begin."

"Why?" I asked.

"Because that way you won't have to tell anyone about it on the playground, and he can tell the class all at once."

"I don't even want to go to school," I said.

"I know. But you have to. And you'll feel better once it's over with. You'll see."

"What about the cage? Should I take it?"

"We'll drop it off another day."

I went to my room and started reading a book but I kept thinking about Bingo and losing my place. I would have played with him all day if only he hadn't died. If Bingo had gone home with someone else, I wondered, would he still be alive? Did he die because I wasn't careful enough? Had I left him in the yard too long when he was used to being inside the classroom? I would have given anything to have him back, alive and healthy.

I rested and hugged my hen and I guess I fell asleep.

◆　◆　◆

On Monday morning I begged Mom to let me stay home from school. "I'll go tomorrow," I said. "Everyone will know about it then."

"It would be just as hard tomorrow," my mother said. "You've got to face it and get it over with today. It won't be as bad as you think, I promise."

I was quiet while Mom drove me to school, even though she kept talking as if it were a regular day. When she pulled up by the school crosswalk and stopped the car, she leaned over to kiss me. I usually think I'm too big to get kisses in front of people, but this day was different.

"See you after school," she said. "I'll be home when you get there."

"Okay."

"I love you, Ellie."

I nodded and didn't answer because I was afraid I might cry. My eyes were wet and I opened them really wide so tears wouldn't run down my face. Sometimes that works, but not this time.

The hall was almost empty as I walked to Room 101. A few of the other classroom doors were already closed.

The door of our room was open and Mr. Garrett was standing beside it. "Good morning, Ellie," he said, as I stepped through the doorway.

"Good morning," I answered, thinking that it was the worst morning of my life.

"Where's Bingo?" Byron yelled.

Before I could speak, Mr. Garrett said, "Take your seat, Ellie. Class, I want your attention."

I sneaked a look at the whole class as I sat down. Everyone was looking at Mr. Garrett except Jenny, who silently mouthed the words to me, "Where's Bingo?"

"Jenny," Mr. Garrett said, "I'd like your attention too. I need to talk to all of you about something quite serious and sad. There has been a loss to this classroom and to the students in it. I'm sorry to say that Bingo died this weekend."

"No," Maria said, and lots of other people began talking at once.

"The rabbit died suddenly and without pain," Mr. Garrett said. "I'm going to tell you about it because, naturally, you'll want to know what happened, and I don't want everyone to have to ask Ellie." He explained what Mom had told him, how Bingo had been playing under the lilac bush, how he hadn't been sick, and he even told how my family and I had buried Bingo in the garden. "We're all sorry that Bingo is gone," he said, "and it will take a while to get used to the idea. But I think it will be easier if we go about our day as usual. Are there any questions at all?"

No one raised a hand and the room was completely silent.

"In that case, class, let's begin our day. I think we'll have about ten minutes of silent reading before our first lesson. If you don't have a book, feel free to take one from the shelf by the window."

I took out my old library book that I'd already finished and I pretended to read.

Maria and Brenda had both been crying while Mr. Garrett talked about Bingo and now they wiped their eyes and opened their books.

No one looked at me and I couldn't tell what anyone was thinking. I knew they were all sad—I was sad too—but I wondered if they blamed me. I was glad that Mr. Garrett had told about Bingo so I didn't have to do it.

By the end of social studies, the classroom seemed more regular. People were talking and sharpening pencils and asking to go to the bathroom.

I still hated to look over at the windowsill and see the box that Dawn had decorated with a picture of Bingo. I wondered if the rest of the class kept looking at it too.

◆ ◆ ◆

It seemed as if everyone except me was buying lunch so they all got to go down first. It was pizza day but I'd forgotten and Mom had made a sandwich for me. I didn't really care about missing pizza since I didn't feel hungry anyway.

Only Adrianne, who's a picky eater, and I carried our lunch boxes down to the cafeteria.

"That's terrible about Bingo," she said.

"Yes," I agreed. "It is."

"I wonder who would have won him?"

"I don't know." I didn't even like to think about it. Somehow remembering that he was going to be someone's personal pet made it worse.

As we walked to the table, I looked at Melissa and remembered how I'd hoped that she'd walk home with me on Friday because I was carrying Bingo's cage. Friday seemed long ago now.

I sat down beside Jenny. Adrianne sat on my other side and she opened up her lunch box.

"Who wants to trade for oatmeal cookies?" she asked.

"Not pizza," Allison said.

"No," Adrianne agreed. "I want that carrot salad."

The cafeteria always serves carrot and raisin salad on pizza day. People either love it or hate it. Adrianne loves it.

"Take mine," Dyonne said, passing her salad down the table. "And I don't like oatmeal cookies."

"You can have mine too," Maria said, handing hers to Melissa, who picked up her own then passed both salads to Adrianne.

"Wow, thanks," Adrianne kept saying, as more salad cups came down the table to her.

I unwrapped my sandwich and took a bite. It was bologna and lettuce, my favorite kind, but it didn't taste that good.

"Ellie," Maria said, "do you think Bingo seemed a little bit sick?"

The table was suddenly quiet.

"No. He wasn't at all," I said. "He was under the lilac bush playing. My brother and I were going to teach him some tricks, then we looked . . . and . . . " I stopped talking.

No one said anything, and I started folding creases in my paper napkin.

"Girls!" Byron screamed, running up to our table. We all jumped because he'd scared us.

"Riddle time, girls," he said, and he had a mean look on his face. He squatted down and gave a few hops. I thought he was going to say something about Melissa liking Frog. Melissa looked away from him and took a bite of her pizza, so I could tell she thought so too.

Then he yelled, "Why is Ellie's mom's restaurant called Pause?"

We all turned around and looked at him. I was relieved that he hadn't said anything about Melissa.

"Give up?" he screeched. "Because they serve rabbit paws. Get it? Paws? If you eat at Pause, you might be eating Bingo."

I put my sandwich down and tried to think of something to say. I felt sick.

"Shut up," Melissa told him.

"Now, Froggy Face," he told her, "you know that rabbits are supposed to be yummy."

"Shut up," Melissa told him again. "Don't you care about anyone, you fat creep?"

"Oh, a hopping mad frog," he said, but he sounded a little embarrassed.

"No one can stand you, Byron," Melissa said, "because you don't care about anyone. Not even Bingo. Everyone loved him. And we all care about Ellie. You're a jerk, Byron. Get away from our table."

"I'll be sure not to let my dog walk past Ellie's house," he said. "I bet Pause cooks dog paws too. Bet there aren't many pets in your neighborhood, Ellie." He walked away.

"He's so mean," Maria said. "Just forget about him, Ellie."

"Yes, forget him," Melissa added.

As sick as I felt about Byron's remarks, I was still happy inside that Melissa had stood up for me.

After lunch, while we were in the middle of the science test, I glanced over at the windowsill and noticed that the box with the picture of Bingo was gone. I decided that Mr. Garrett had put it up in the storeroom or maybe he'd thrown it in the trash. I was glad he'd taken it away.

During health, I saw Byron pass a note to Bruce. Bruce read it, looked at me, and laughed. I knew it was one of Byron's jokes about the restaurant. I wondered how many boys had laughed about it during lunch. I hoped Wallace hadn't laughed.

I saw Bruce pass Byron's note back to Scott. Then Scott read it and passed it to Wallace, but I didn't watch enough to see if they were laughing at me the way Bruce had. Mr. Garrett didn't see the note going around and I was glad because I didn't want to hear it read out loud.

We were supposed to take our art folders home from school that day. Any art projects that hadn't been taken home during the year, like the ones that had been used on bulletin boards and some that had been part of the set for the first-grade play, had been put into folders. My folder was huge.

I balanced my school books, my art folder, and my lunch box as I walked down the hall after the bell rang.

"I'll help you if you want," Melissa said, coming up beside me.

"Oh. Thanks," I said, looking over at her. She wasn't carrying a lunch box or any school books, and her art folder was smaller than mine.

"I'll carry your books," she said, reaching over for them.

I let them go and put my lunch box on top of my art folder.

"That's better," I said. "Thanks."

We didn't talk as we left the building and started down the street. After the first block Melissa didn't take the shortcut, so I knew that she was going to walk me all the way home.

"Melissa," I said, taking a deep breath. "I'm sorry we fought."

"So am I," she answered.

"What I'm really sorry for is telling Dawn that you like Frog. Joey. I shouldn't have."

"Okay," she said. And I knew we were friends again.

"I still like Wallace," I said, giving her a secret.

"I still like Joey."

"I won't tell one of your secrets again," I promised. "Ever."

She nodded her head to show she believed me.

"I wonder if Wallace thinks the things Byron says about Bingo are funny," I said. "Did you see them all passing notes?"

"Yes. Byron had about three notes that he sent around to the boys. The boys hardly ever get caught passing notes."

"But they don't send them as often as we do," I said. "The girls send them way more, that's why we get caught more."

"Maybe so."

We got to my house and Melissa handed my books back.

"Can you come over?" I asked.

"I have piano," she said.

"Oh, yeah." I had forgotten that she takes piano every Monday. It seemed as though we hadn't been together for such a long time.

"I'll come by for you tomorrow," she said.

"Okay. Thanks for carrying these. Tell Gayle hello."

When I got into the house, I washed out my thermos and put it in the cupboard. I made two peanut-butter-and-jelly sandwiches, one for me and one as a surprise for Jake. I put his sandwich in a plastic bag.

I sat down at the kitchen table and began my science homework as I ate.

Mom arrived before I finished the last problem.

"So how did it go?" she asked, sitting down across from me.

"It was okay," I said. "And Mom, Melissa and I are friends. We made up."

"That's such good news. I was so worried about you, and then I got caught in traffic so I'm late. And now you have good news." She smiled. "I feel better now."

"I do too. I made Jake a surprise sandwich. Do you want half?"

"No, thanks. I want a cup of coffee, as I sit here and hear all about how you and Melissa made up."

I stood up. "I'll be the waitress," I said, which is something I've said since I was little.

"And I'll be the customer," Mom said. "With pleasure."

11

The next day was Sue Ann's first day back after the chicken pox. When I saw her on the playground before school I felt kind of annoyed and surprised. It was almost as though I'd forgotten about her, though, of course, I knew she'd be back. It wasn't as if she moved away or anything. But I hated the thought of telling her about Bingo. For once, I hoped Melissa had been talking to her.

She had. Sue Ann rushed over to me as soon as she saw me.

"Ellie," she said, "Melissa told me about Bingo. I'm sorry that happened."

"Yes. Everybody's sad that he's gone."

"Well, yes, that too. But what I mean is, I'm sorry it happened to you. At your house." She put her hand on my arm. "I'm really sorry," she said again, and I could tell that she meant it.

"Thank you," I said. "Thanks. Are you well now?"

"Yes. And glad to be back."

"I'm glad you are too." I almost meant it and that surprised me.

Jenny, Melissa, Sue Ann, and I stood around the tetherball pole waiting our turn. Byron ran by and yelled out to Bruce, "Eating rabbits' paws brings good luck!"

"What does he mean?" Sue Ann asked me.

"He's acting as if we did something terrible to Bingo," I said.

"I know that part," she answered, "but what about bringing luck? What does he mean?"

"Rabbits' feet are supposed to be lucky. Once I saw someone with a key chain made out of one. It was dyed green."

"That's terrible," Sue Ann said.

"I know."

Byron and Bruce came up closer when they saw that they had a larger audience. Some kids from other classrooms were gathered around the tetherball pole with us, hoping for a turn before the bell rang.

"You know, Ellie," Byron said, "I probably would have been the one to get Bingo if you hadn't let him die."

I didn't answer.

"Yeah," Bruce said. "Way to go, Ellie. Thanks a lot." The bell rang then and both boys walked off. Everyone else picked up their books and lunch sacks from the ground.

"Just ignore them," Melissa told me. "They

wouldn't have even been in the drawing if Ms. Simpson was here. They wouldn't have won."

I knew Melissa was being nice and trying to make me feel better. But still it was true that they might have won, any of us might have, and I couldn't help wondering whether Bingo would still be alive if he hadn't come home with me. Maybe they were rude enough to say what a lot of other people were thinking. I couldn't be sure.

The last person in each row passes out the math workbooks, so Byron passed them out to the row beside me. When he arrived at Donna's desk, he handed the green-and-yellow book to her and at the same time, he leaned over and said to me, "Thanks a lot, Ellie. You killed my rabbit."

I looked down at my own math workbook, which Jenny had put on my desk, and I pretended not to hear him. I was both mad and sad. I wanted to say something back, something mean, but I also felt sad that I'd taken away everyone's chance to win Bingo, even my own chance.

We worked on mixed numbers, which I don't hate, and the time until lunch passed quickly. When Byron came back up his row collecting workbooks, I pretended I was busy leaning under my desk to get out my lunch box.

As I sat up, I saw the note on my desk. It was folded like a greeting card. On the front it said, "Thanks," and there was a picture that I knew was supposed to be Bingo. Before I could open the card, Mr. Garrett took it out of my hand and walked back to the front of the classroom.

"This note was given to Ellie by Byron," he said. He looked at the front of the card and then opened it. I held my breath because I knew what it was going to say, something about how it was my fault that Bingo died.

Mr. Garrett took a long time to read the inside of the card. Then he closed it, put it on his desk, and covered it with his lesson plan book.

Everyone was quiet. Mr. Garrett had always read notes out loud immediately, as soon as he picked them up. I wished he'd go ahead and get it over with because waiting was making my stomach hurt.

For a moment I thought he was going to write on the chalkboard. He held a piece of chalk in his fingers, turning it over and over, and at last he spoke.

"The note I picked up indicates we're having a problem in this classroom that I hoped we could avoid. The note tells me that some of us blame Ellie for Bingo's death."

No one moved in their seats. I looked down at my desk top. I'd known that's what the note was going to say but, somehow, it seemed worse when Mr. Garrett said it out loud.

"I knew of a similar problem once. There was a

lady who was quite ill. Quite ill." He paused and I thought of Ms. Simpson's mother. "She was in the hospital and she wasn't expected to live much longer," Mr. Garrett continued. "Her husband stayed with her as much as he could." Mr. Garrett paused and looked at the chalk. "Then one evening the lady's doctor, who was a family friend, encouraged the husband to go home from the hospital to rest a bit. But the husband was afraid to leave his wife, afraid she might get worse. The doctor, their friend, insisted that she'd be fine for those few hours and he urged the husband to go." Mr. Garrett paused again. He seemed to be thinking. "So I left," he said. "And while I was gone, my wife died."

I was shocked, and I stared at Mr. Garrett, who kept speaking.

"My friend, the doctor, called and told me what had happened. He said he was sorry and he felt bad that he'd encouraged me to leave. And I knew he felt bad. But I still blamed him for it. It was as if I blamed him for everything. My wife's death, my own sadness, everything. It took me two months to see what I was doing. So I'd not only lost my dear wife, which was no one's fault, but for two months I'd also lost my friend, which was my own fault. Does anyone see what I'm trying to tell you?"

No one raised a hand. No one made a sound.

"What I'm saying is that some people—very few,

I'm sure—are blaming Ellie for something that we're all sad about but that was not her fault. She did her best. Her family did their best. And their best was very good indeed. If there's anyone here who thinks he or she could have done a better job of taking care of the rabbit, who could have given it a gentler farewell, please raise your hand."

No hands went up.

"You must stop blaming Ellie. Today. Right now. Is that clear? Her good-bye to Bingo was from all of us. And a decent good-bye it was." He was silent for a moment and then he said, "If there are no questions, we will have free reading until the lunch bell rings." No hands were raised. Mr. Garrett said, "Fine," took his seat, and opened his lesson plan book.

Slowly, people in the class opened their desks and took out their library books. I took mine out and read the same page over and over until the lunch bell rang.

Almost the entire class left at the first bell because the cafeteria was serving tacos. Jenny, Melissa, and Sue Ann walked beside me. No one said anything for a few minutes.

Then Melissa said, "I wonder what illness Mr. Garrett's wife had."

"I don't know," Jenny said. "Mr. Garrett seemed sad, huh?"

"Yes," Melissa agreed. "I wonder when she died.

That was good, Ellie, the way he told those boys not to blame you. He's nice now, I think. Anyway, I like him."

Jenny spoke. "Remember when you wrote that about him on the board, Ellie?"

I nodded. If she remembered, I knew Mr. Garrett remembered. So much had changed since then, at least for me.

Byron and Bruce passed us in the hall. They didn't say anything mean or act silly, they just kept walking. I was glad.

After lunch, out on the playground, Byron came over to the swings where Melissa and I were talking.

"Ellie," he said.

I turned toward him, afraid of what he might say.

"What page do we have for science?" he asked.

I thought for a moment. "Two fourteen," I said. "The Let's Practice section."

"Okay," he said, and he walked off.

"I'm going to faint," Melissa said.

"Me too," I told her. "I wonder why he did that? Does that mean he might stop being awful about Bingo?"

"I don't know. Maybe he's just trying to imitate a normal human being," she said.

"Well, he'll have to work on the body," I said.

"True," she answered, just as the bell rang.

◆ ◆ ◆

"Do you think it helped?" Dad asked. "With the boys who were bothering you?"

"Yes. It was mostly Byron. And Bruce. I didn't hear anyone else. Anyway, Byron stopped and Bruce does anything that Byron does, so he'll stop too."

"That's good," Dad said.

"Mr. Garrett also told us about his wife dying," I said. "And how he blamed the doctor but shouldn't have."

Mom looked at Dad. "I wonder if he should be talking about that in school," she asked.

"We're not babies, Mom. He doesn't treat us like babies."

I felt mad. Mr. Garrett thought we were old enough to understand, and he was right, we were. He wouldn't say something too old for us. He knew us. I looked at Dad. "He was *trying* to show us that it's wrong to blame people. Do *you* get it, Dad?"

"I get the fact that you're being rude to your mother, and I want it to stop," my father answered, and he wasn't joking.

I didn't talk at all for the rest of dinner. Later, when I was doing the dishes, Mom came and helped dry.

12

*T*wo weeks later, summer seemed very close, and the time was passing quickly. We had projects in school that we had to finish, and everyone was working on our final school program during any free time.

On Monday of the last week of school, after English, Mr. Garrett said that he had an announcement to make.

"We need to make some plans, as a class, for a class party on Friday," he said.

Lots of people cheered. Some classes have parties, but not all. It's up to the teachers. I was a little surprised about Mr. Garrett deciding to have one. Surprised but happy.

"We can talk about your ideas," he said, "and what you might want to have to eat and so on. I'm going to leave all the plans up to you. After all, you're essentially sixth-graders now. Who would like to keep track of the plans by writing on the board?"

Sue Ann's hand went up, and then everyone's hand followed, some people calling, "Me, me!"

"I believe I saw Sue Ann first," Mr. Garrett said.

He handed the chalk to her and then said, "I'd like to bring up the first new order of business before I turn the floor over to all of you. We will have a drawing for a new pet that I think everyone will come to enjoy. Another note will be required from your parents granting permission, and the drawing will be held this Friday at the class party."

Everyone started talking at once. I looked over to where Bingo's cage had been, but nothing was there.

"I'll go get him now," Mr. Garrett said. "He's in the teachers' lounge. Naturally, I'll expect order while I'm gone. Sue Ann, perhaps you could start leading a discussion of the class party."

He left the room and we all started chattering.

"Maybe it's a kitten," Maria said. "I'd like that."

I remembered that Mr. Garrett had picked the cage up at my house soon after Bingo died. I hadn't been home when he came for it. I wondered if the new pet would fit in that cage. Maybe it was a dog. I was pretty sure my parents wouldn't sign for a dog.

The door opened and Mr. Garrett came in carrying Bingo's cage and saying, "Here we go, class." His face was a little pink, and it was obvious that he was excited.

There was a rabbit in the cage, a rabbit much smaller than Bingo. It had long, gray fur.

"Let's keep our seats," Mr. Garrett said, "so we don't scare him. I'll put him on the desk so we all can get a good look."

Everyone raved about how cute and tiny he was.

"What's his name?" Dawn asked.

"That will be up to you as a class," Mr. Garrett said. "You can decide that as you plan the party. I'll take a seat in the back and work on these papers. If you need assistance, just ask. Sue Ann, you're in charge now."

"Shall we name the rabbit first?" Sue Ann asked the class, and we all said yes.

The rabbit hopped around in the cage on Mr. Garrett's desk as we named him. Once in a while, he would rest and munch on a wedge of cabbage or drink from his water bottle.

The final choices for names came down to Dusty and Thumper. Most people thought that Thumper sounded too babyish so Dusty won.

We voted on who would get to take care of Dusty at recess during the week. When Ms. Simpson had first brought Bingo to school, we didn't let him loose at recess. We held him in our laps outside, so he'd get used to the playground and noise. Now we decided that Dusty would be held by two people each day, and he wouldn't be put down outside because we couldn't be sure that he'd be tame enough not to run away. Whoever won him for good could tame him at home.

"Now, about the party," Sue Ann said. "What shall we have to eat?"

We all agreed on hamburgers and hot dogs. Mr. Garrett said that we could go to the park for our picnic and that he'd cook the food there. "I can't promise excellent results," he said. "It's been a while, but I'll give it a try."

"I'll bring fudge," Melissa said.

Wallace and Ben volunteered lemonade, and they said that they each had a large thermos that their parents would let them use.

I said I'd bring chocolate chip cookies, and so did Jenny. If there were any leftovers, we figured people could take them home.

It didn't take long to plan the entire party, down to who would bring the paper cups and napkins. The only thing that Mr. Garrett had to bring was the charcoal for the barbecue. We'd finished the party plans and were doing math when Mr. Garrett got called to the office on the intercom.

"I'd like order while I'm gone, class," he said.

The moment he left, Melissa stood up and said, "What do you think about each of us chipping in a dollar to buy Mr. Garrett a present?"

"Good. Great," people answered. I thought it sounded fine.

"Is it okay if Ellie and I pick it out?" she asked, and everyone agreed again. I was glad she chose me.

"Good. Then give me your money when you can, but not in front of Mr. Garrett. Try to bring it tomorrow. And if you have any ideas for the present, tell me or Ellie. We'll have it ready for the class party."

She had just sat back down when Mr. Garrett returned.

"Let's begin the quiz section," he said. "All books open to two thirty-three."

◆　◆　◆

We had practiced a lot for our end-of-school program. We were supposed to combine the program with the award ceremony on Wednesday and the awards would be given first.

The class awards are never much of a surprise to us because we all know who's good at what subject and who did special projects during the year. But it's fun to see your friends go up for an award and it's nice if you get to go up yourself. I got one award, for social studies, and I saw my parents smiling at me as I walked up to accept it. I knew where they were sitting because I'd spotted them when our class filed into the gym. I can remember, in younger grades, how we'd all look for our parents and wave at them and some kids would even call out to them. In fifth grade we still look for them, but we don't make it so noticeable. I just smiled when I saw mine and didn't wave.

After the award ceremony, there was a ten-minute intermission while students left to put on their costumes for the program.

Our class was going to sing three songs, two in English about spring and one German song that told about the birds returning in the springtime. Mr. Garrett had taught it to us and we knew what the words meant, but most people probably wouldn't.

To help people understand the German song, Dawn had painted a large, flat tree on cardboard stapled to wood, and two pieces of wood formed a stand at the bottom. Dawn was supposed to carry the tree on stage before the song started. During the song, ten of us were to bring out paper birds that we'd drawn and cut out and we were supposed to stick them in the tree as the song was being performed. I was the third person, and it was a little embarrassing for me to walk up, still singing, and stick my robin on the tree. I was afraid that the people in front could hear my voice too much while I was up there. Back at my own place, I saw Allison go up and come back and then it was Shannon's turn. I didn't see how Shannon stuck her bird on. Maybe she pushed the tree too hard, but all of a sudden the whole tree crashed to the floor. Paper leaves and paper birds flew everywhere. At the end of the song, the audience clapped and cheered and also laughed a little but not in a mean way. Mr. Garrett and Dawn carried the tree off stage.

"I don't know what happened," I heard her say to Mr. Garrett. "Did I put the boards on wrong?"

"No, it was fine," he said. "It was fine. Don't worry."

"Did it ruin our part?" Dawn sounded near tears.

Mr. Garrett put his hand on her shoulder. "Your work enhanced our part. And you dealt with the unforeseen quickly and well. Fine job."

After the program, the parents were invited to get cookies and juice at the back of the gym. As soon as all the adults were served, the students got in line. Everyone had found their parents right away.

"Wasn't that awful about the tree?" I asked when I spotted Mom and Dad.

"Not that bad," Dad said. "They handled it fine."

"And the song was lovely," Mom added.

"Hello, Mr. and Mrs. Brader," Sue Ann said, walking up to my parents. "I'm so happy that you could come."

"Thank you, Sue Ann," my mother said. "We enjoyed the performance."

"Looking forward to summer?" Dad asked her.

"Yes, I am. But, of course, I'll miss school terribly."

My parents nodded and smiled as Sue Ann walked away. Out of our whole class, only Sue Ann would say that she'd miss school terribly. Some people get bored toward the end of summer and are glad when school starts, but no one plans ahead of time to miss school except Sue Ann.

I told my parents that Mr. Garrett said we could take our parents to the classroom to see Dusty if they were undecided about whether they wanted to sign for him or not.

"But we already sent your note," Mom said.

"I know. But he means that anyone can see him. Do you want to?"

"Sure," Dad said. "Lead the way."

Wallace and his parents and Jenny and her mother were looking at Dusty when we arrived.

"Is he as tame as the first one?" Wallace's mother asked.

"No," Wallace said. "Not yet. But he will be."

"He's very pretty," Mom said, reaching out to brush her hand against the cage where his fur was sticking out. Dusty didn't move away.

"He's getting tamer already," Wallace said.

"Well," Jenny's mother said, "he'll be a nice pet for someone."

"I hope us," Jenny said.

"That would be fine," her mother told her.

◆ ◆ ◆

Most kids in the class brought money for Mr. Garrett's present. We had twenty-four dollars because

Maria gave extra. The only suggestion was made by Shannon who said, "What about a fishing pole?" but we didn't know if he fished or how much a pole would cost.

During dinner, after the school program, I described Dusty to Jake.

"He's beautiful," I told him. "Gray and fluffy."

"How many kids in your class?" Jake asked me.

"Twenty-two."

"How many will draw for him?"

"Probably about twenty. Shannon's dad is mean."

"So the odds are twenty to one," he said. "Not so hot. But someone has to win. Is Mr. Garrett in the drawing?"

"No," I said. "Well, I guess not. I never thought of it. But I'm sure he just bought Dusty for us. Because of Bingo."

"I thought he was too mean for that," Jake said.

"He's not mean," I said.

"You kept telling us how mean he was, how he wasn't as nice as Ms. Simpson, how he wasn't fair. Right, Mom? Dad?"

My parents didn't answer.

"That was before I knew him," I said.

"More potatoes, anyone?" Mom asked, picking up the serving bowl.

"Yes," Jake said, reaching out his hand.

Mom didn't let go of the bowl.

"Yes, please," he said.

She handed the bowl to him.

"There's more salad, if anyone's interested," she said.

No one was, but both Jake and I said, "No, thank you," just the way Dad did, and Mom looked pleased.

13

*M*y mother dropped us off at Goodwater's gift shop so we could look for Mr. Garrett's gift. There were three of us, because we'd invited Jenny when she said that she wished she could come along.

A saleswoman at Goodwater's had shown us a few things, but none of them seemed right. After a while we said that we'd look by ourselves and call her if we found something.

"I wish we could afford this," Jenny said pointing to a wooden dart board that folded into a cabinet. It cost $66.00.

"It's pretty," Melissa said, "but maybe he doesn't play darts."

"I think it's mostly for decoration," Jenny said, and I agreed.

"My mom said that wooden boxes are nice for

presents," I told my friends. "My uncle collects them."

Goodwater's had shelves of wooden boxes, each one with a tag that said what kind of wood it was made of.

"It's hard to decide with all this here," Melissa said.

"Maybe we should choose the card first," Jenny said.

The teacher cards were mostly birthday cards, so we found a regular good-bye card that said inside, "We'll miss you."

"Perfect," Melissa said. "That's a dollar fifty of our money gone, though."

We went back to look at the wooden boxes some more and that's when Jenny saw it. There were two, really. Two china rabbits that were so realistic you could almost see their noses wiggling. One was a white rabbit munching on a carrot, and the other one, the one that was watching a bee, looked exactly like Bingo.

We all stared at it. "I don't know," Jenny said. "Would that be sad? Would that make him sad?"

"Does it make you sad?" Melissa asked her.

"No. I like it. It looks so much like Bingo."

"It does," I said. "I think it's the best thing. But how much is it?"

Jenny picked the statue up and turned it over. It cost $11.95.

"We'll even have some left," Melissa said. "Why don't we buy him candy with the rest?" We chose a box of assorted chocolates.

Then the saleswoman wrapped the presents in tulip paper. She held different ribbons up against the wrapped boxes so we could choose the ones that matched best with the tulips. I really like store people who are nice like that, even to kids.

On Friday, Melissa brought the presents to school in a grocery bag so Mr. Garrett wouldn't see them. On the playground before the bell, we told everyone in class what the presents were and had them sign the card.

Back in the classroom that afternoon, we sat at our desks eating chocolate chip cookies. Everyone had stuffed themselves on toasted marshmallows at the park, so we'd voted to eat the cookies in our room. Even though the barbecue was lots of fun, we'd all been anxious to get back to class to see who won Dusty.

"Well," Mr. Garrett said, "I guess we'd better get down to the last few items of business, and then we'll call it a year. Is everyone ready to draw for the rabbit?"

We all cheered, and Byron whistled.

"Shall I get someone from another room to draw, or will you trust me?" Mr. Garrett asked.

"You do it." "You." "We trust you."

"All right, then. Ben, why don't you give that box at least fifteen good shakes and then let me pick."

We all counted out loud as Ben shook the box hard. The folded permission slips clunked as they tumbled around inside.

"Okay, Ben," Mr. Garrett said, "take the lid off."

When Ben removed the lid, Mr. Garrett looked away so he couldn't see into the box. He reached in and took out a paper.

"And the winner is . . ." Byron said, with a nervous laugh.

Mr. Garrett unfolded the slip of paper and looked at it.

"Dusty's owner," he said, "is Maria Randolph."

There was a second of silence before everyone began to applaud.

"Oh, oh, oh!" Maria said, bouncing up and down in her chair.

"Do you have anything you want to say?" Mr. Garrett asked her, when the applause stopped.

"Yes," she said. "You can all come and see him anytime. You can be his aunts and uncles."

We laughed and applauded again.

"Thank you," Mr. Garrett told Maria. "I'm sure many of us will take you up on that offer."

Melissa raised her hand.

"Melissa?" Mr. Garrett said.

She stood up. "Mr. Garrett, Room 101 has a present that we would like to give to you. It's from all of us."

"Oh, my. I certainly can't argue with that," he said. "How kind of you."

Melissa stepped forward carrying her grocery bag. She reached in and took out the card first and handed it to Mr. Garrett.

"This is a surprise, I assure you," he said as he opened the envelope. He read the words to the card out loud and then he also read each person's name, looking at each of us after he said our names. "Thank you," he said, at the end.

Next Melissa gave him the box of candy. As the paper came off, he said, "I'll have to share these with my friends. Bev, will you pass them around?"

Melissa handed him the rabbit box last. He took the tissue paper out of the box carefully and then he lifted out the rabbit. "How kind," he said, holding up the gift. "In memory of our absent friend. Thank you very much."

Mr. Garrett sat down at his desk, and when the candy came back around to him, he chose a piece and told us how delicious it was.

"Now," he said, standing up, "I think I'd better say a few words about report cards, which I'll pass out to you in a few moments when you leave."

We all groaned.

"One, you may keep these at home. Your parents

do not have to return them. The other thing is, it seems that every year that I've taught, at the end of the year, I'd always hear students asking each other if they passed to the next grade. So I'd like to announce that every student in this room is now a sixth- grader. Congratulations."

Byron led the applause this time. I think he was relieved.

"One final word before we file out. You'll notice that I put my address on the back of each of your report cards. I would like to hear from you in the future. I'd like to hear of your accomplishments, which I know will be forthcoming." He paused for a moment. "I'd also like to say that the chance to teach this class came at a time when I particularly needed it, and it has been a wonderful experience for me. It's been my pleasure. Room 101, class is dismissed. Collect your report cards at the door."

He shook each person's hand as he gave us our report cards.

"Have a good summer, Ellie," he said, squeezing my hand.

I nodded but I didn't really look at him because I felt like crying to be leaving him for good.

Melissa's mother picked her up to go shopping for camp, so I had no one to walk home with. I hung around outside the building for a few minutes and then decided that I was going back in to talk to Mr. Garrett. I wasn't sure what I wanted to say. I knew that I could never apologize for writing about him on the board that day. And I sure couldn't tell him that I hadn't liked him at first but now I did. But I thought that, as a sixth-grader, maybe I could think of something mature to say that would give him the idea.

The closer I got to the classroom, the more I realized that I didn't know what to say, but I still wasn't willing just to give up.

I stopped by the doorway, took a deep breath, and walked into the room.

It was empty. There were a few chocolate chip cookies left on a plate on Mr. Garrett's desk, along with the open box of candy. The rabbit statue was gone. He must have taken it with him, I thought, maybe to the office or to the teachers' lounge.

I was sort of relieved to see the room empty, but I was a little sad too. It was so quiet without any of the class there. The room itself looked lonely. I had never been in the room alone except for the time I had to stay in and clean the boards.

I looked at my desk for a moment, and then I turned to leave. But before I got to the door I stopped, went back, and picked up the eraser.

I cleaned the boards the way Mr. Garrett had taught us to, first using the regular eraser and then the chamois one. Then I drew a heart on the board as perfectly as I could. I drew it beside the place where Mr. Garrett had written the date that morning. Inside the heart I printed, "Ellie Brader Loves Mr. G."

Maybe he won't even notice it, I thought, putting the chalk down. Maybe someone else would erase the board and Mr. Garrett would never see it. But then again, maybe he would.

I walked out of the room and down the hall. As I opened the door to the building and stepped outside, the spring air felt warm, like the beginning of summer. I took my time walking home.

About the Author

JANET JOHNSTON was born in Pittsburgh, Pennsylvania. The daughter of an air force officer, she lived in many different places throughout her childhood. She received a B.S. degree in English and education from Southwest Texas State University. Currently she lives in Panama, where she teaches high-school English for the U.S. Department of Defense Dependents Schools. Her husband, Wallace Teal, is a fire chief for the Panama Canal Commission. Their four grown children live in the States.

Aside from writing—admittedly her favorite pastime—Janet Johnston's favorite activities are reading, watching movies, having dinner with friends, and playing with her pets. *Ellie Brader Hates Mr. G.* is her first book.